DISNEY · PIXAR

INCREDIBLES 2

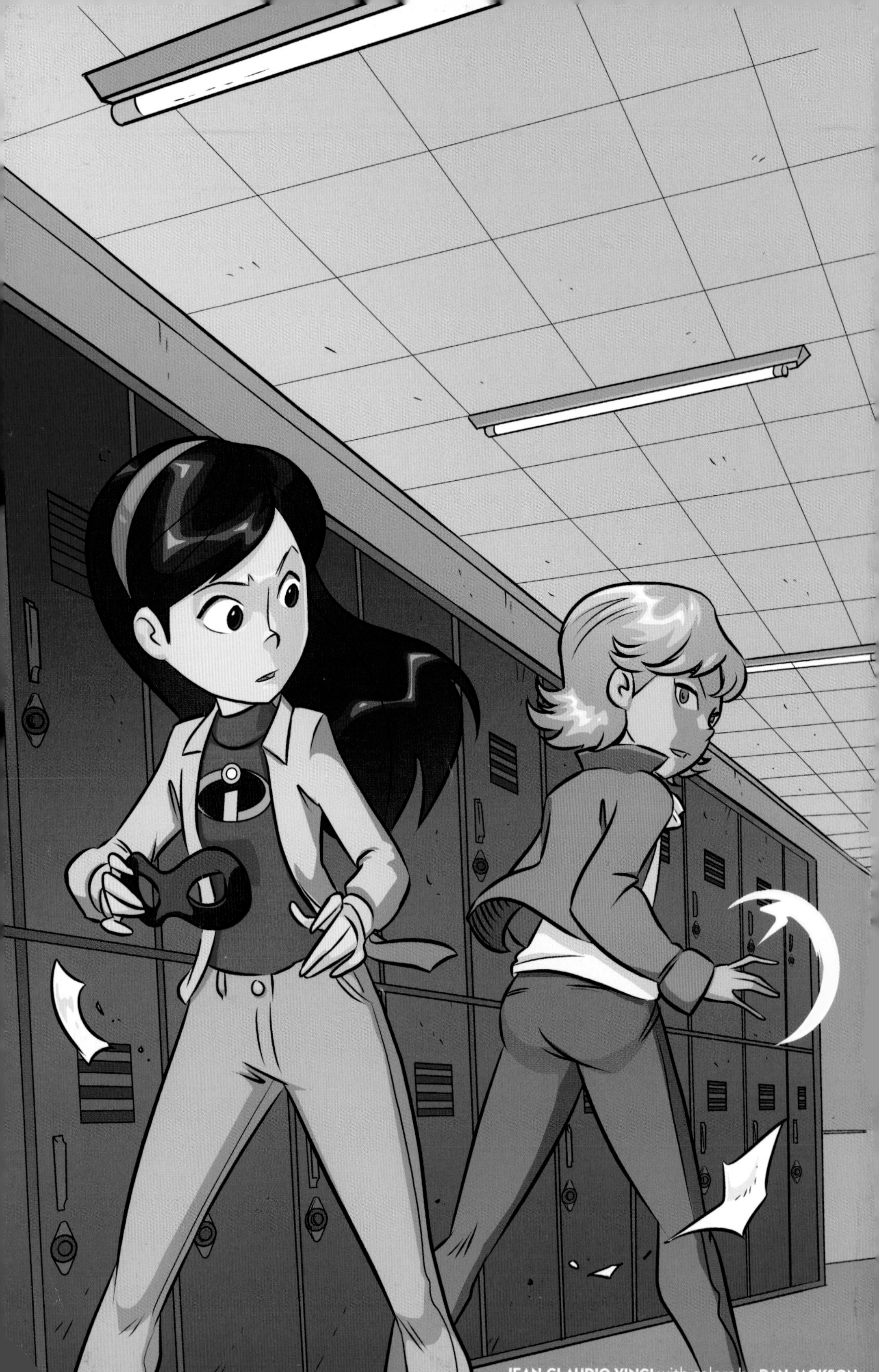

JEAN-CLAUDIO VINCI with colors by **DAN JACKSON**

Disney · PIXAR
INCREDIBLES 2

SECRET IDENTITIES

Script
CHRISTOS GAGE

Art & Cover
JEAN-CLAUDIO VINCI

Color Art
DAN JACKSON

Lettering
RICHARD STARKINGS &
COMICRAFT'S JIMMY BETANCOURT

DARK HORSE BOOKS

DARK HORSE BOOKS

president and publisher
MIKE RICHARDSON

editor
FREDDYE MILLER AND SHANTEL LaROCQUE

assistant editor
JUDY KHUU AND BRETT ISRAEL

designer
DAVID NESTELLE

digital art technician
CHRISTIANNE GILLENARDO-GOUDREAU

Neil Hankerson Executive Vice President • Tom Weddle Chief Financial Officer • Randy Stradley Vice President of Publishing • Nick McWhorter Chief Business Development Officer • Dale LaFountain Chief Information Officer • Matt Parkinson Vice President of Marketing • Cara Niece Vice President of Production and Scheduling • Mark Bernardi Vice President of Book Trade and Digital Sales • Ken Lizzi General Counsel • Dave Marshall Editor in Chief • Davey Estrada Editorial Director • Chris Warner Senior Books Editor • Cary Grazzini Director of Specialty Projects • Lia Ribacchi Art Director • Vanessa Todd-Holmes Director of Print Purchasing • Matt Dryer Director of Digital Art and Prepress • Michael Gombos Senior Director of Licensed Publications • Kari Yadro Director of Custom Programs • Kari Torson Director of International Licensing • Sean Brice Director of Trade Sales

DISNEY PUBLISHING WORLDWIDE GLOBAL MAGAZINES, COMICS AND PARTWORKS

PUBLISHER Lynn Waggoner • EDITORIAL TEAM Bianca Coletti (Director, Magazines), Guido Frazzini (Director, Comics), Carlotta Quattrocolo (Executive Editor), Stefano Ambrosio (Executive Editor, New IP), Camilla Vedove (Senior Manager, Editorial Development), Behnoosh Khalili (Senior Editor), Julie Dorris (Senior Editor), Mina Riazi (Assistant Editor), Jonathan Manning (Assistant Editor) • DESIGN Enrico Soave (Senior Designer) • ART Ken Shue (VP, Global Art), Manny Mederos (Senior Illustration Manager, Comics and Magazines), Roberto Santillo (Creative Director), Marco Ghiglione (Creative Manager), Stefano Attardi (Computer Art Designer) • PORTFOLIO MANAGEMENT Olivia Ciancarelli (Director) • BUSINESS & MARKETING Mariantonietta Galla (Marketing Manager), Virpi Korhonen (Editorial Manager)

INCREDIBLES 2: SECRET IDENTITIES

Library of Congress Cataloging-in-Publication Data

Names: Gage, Christos, author. | Vinci, Jean-Claudio, artist. | Jackson, Dan,
 1971- colourist. | Starkings, Richard, letterer. | Betancourt, Jimmy,
 letterer.
Title: Secret identities / script, Christos Gage ; art & cover, Jean-Claudio
 Vinci ; color art, Dan Jackson ; lettering, Richard Starkings &
 Comicraft's Jimmy Betancourt.
Other titles: Incredibles 2 (Motion picture)
Description: First edition. | Milwaukie, OR : Dark Horse Books, 2019. |
 "Disney - PIXAR Incredibles 2."
Identifiers: LCCN 2019015200 | ISBN 9781506713922
Classification: LCC PZ7.7.G25 Sec 2019 | DDC 741.5/973--dc23
LC record available at https://lccn.loc.gov/2019015200

Published by Dark Horse Books
A division of Dark Horse Comics, LLC
10956 SE Main Street
Milwaukie, OR 97222

DarkHorse.com

To find a comics shop in your area, visit comicshoplocator.com

First edition: September 2019
ISBN 978-1-50671-392-2
Digital ISBN 978-1-50671-393-9

1 3 5 7 9 10 8 6 4 2
Printed in China

MEET THE PARR FAMILY—AKA . . .
THE INCREDIBLES!

BOB PARR "MR. INCREDIBLE"

Married to Elastigirl and father of three growing Supers, Bob has found that parenting is a truly heroic act. He has the power of mega-strength and invulnerability—and also an uncanny ability to sense danger.

HELEN PARR "ELASTIGIRL"

While she kept her hero identity dormant for years while taking on parenting, Helen was one of the best Supers in her heyday. She has the power to bend, stretch, and twist into any form.

VIOLET PARR

The oldest of the three Parr children. Fourteen years old, she is intelligent, sarcastic, and a little socially awkward—but she isn't afraid to speak her mind. Violet has the power to become invisible and create force fields.

DASHIELL "DASH" PARR

The middle child in the Parr family. Ten years old, he is adventurous, curious, competitive, and a little bit of a show-off. Dash has the power of super speed, and he doesn't want to hold back using it!

JACK-JACK PARR

In many ways he is a typical toddler—he talks baby-talk, makes messes at mealtime, and gets into things he shouldn't—but Jack-Jack is actually a polymorph and has an array of super powers.

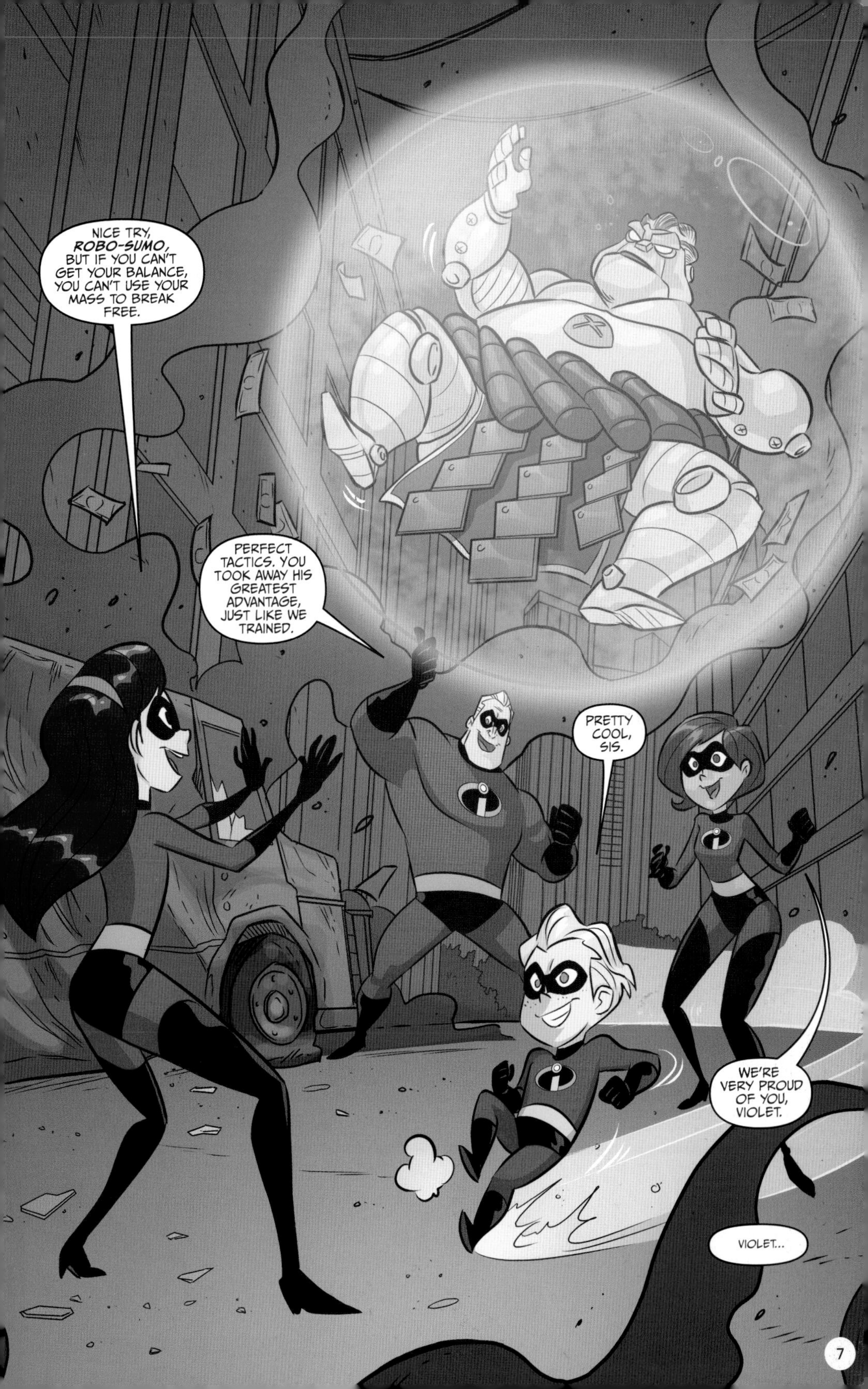
NICE TRY, **ROBO-SUMO**, BUT IF YOU CAN'T GET YOUR BALANCE, YOU CAN'T USE YOUR MASS TO BREAK FREE.
PERFECT TACTICS. YOU TOOK AWAY HIS GREATEST ADVANTAGE, JUST LIKE WE TRAINED.
PRETTY COOL, SIS.
WE'RE VERY PROUD OF YOU, VIOLET.
VIOLET...

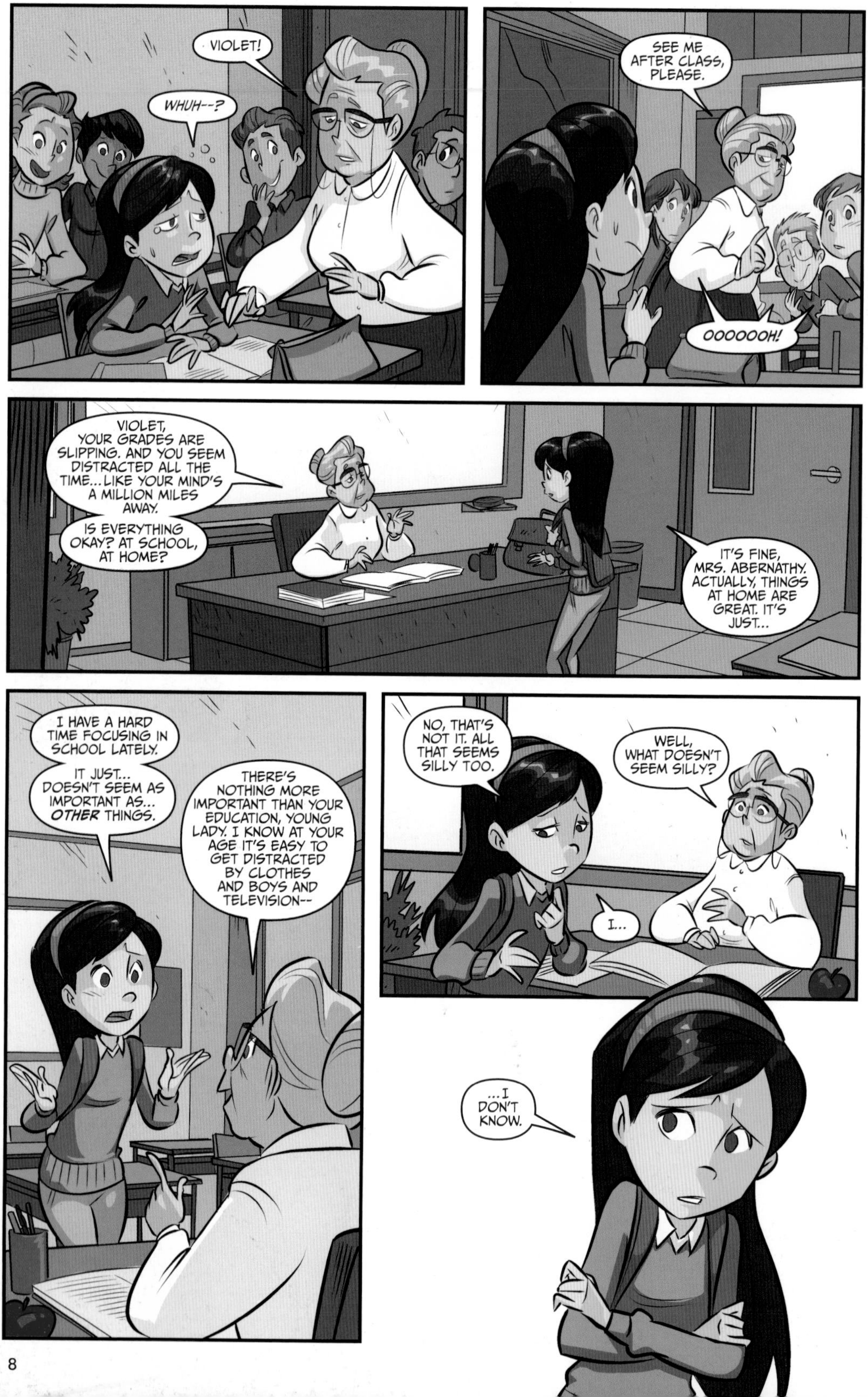
VIOLET!
WHUH--?
SEE ME AFTER CLASS, PLEASE.
OOOOOOH!
VIOLET, YOUR GRADES ARE SLIPPING. AND YOU SEEM DISTRACTED ALL THE TIME...LIKE YOUR MIND'S A MILLION MILES AWAY.
IS EVERYTHING OKAY? AT SCHOOL, AT HOME?
IT'S FINE, MRS. ABERNATHY. ACTUALLY, THINGS AT HOME ARE GREAT. IT'S JUST...
I HAVE A HARD TIME FOCUSING IN SCHOOL LATELY.
IT JUST... DOESN'T SEEM AS IMPORTANT AS... OTHER THINGS.
THERE'S NOTHING MORE IMPORTANT THAN YOUR EDUCATION, YOUNG LADY. I KNOW AT YOUR AGE IT'S EASY TO GET DISTRACTED BY CLOTHES AND BOYS AND TELEVISION--
NO, THAT'S NOT IT. ALL THAT SEEMS SILLY TOO.
WELL, WHAT DOESN'T SEEM SILLY?
I...
...I DON'T KNOW.

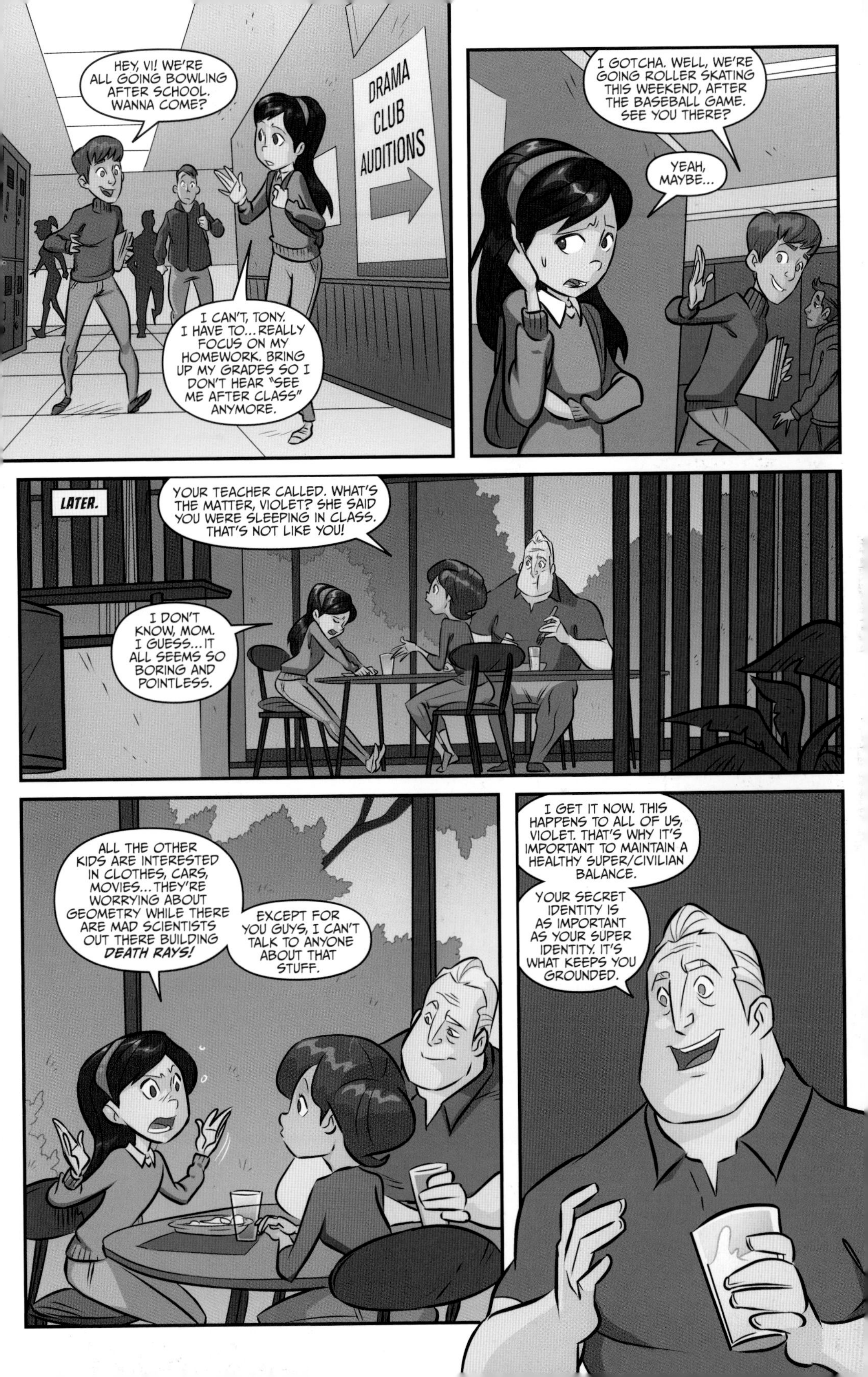
HEY, VI! WE'RE ALL GOING BOWLING AFTER SCHOOL. WANNA COME?
DRAMA CLUB AUDITIONS
I CAN'T, TONY. I HAVE TO... REALLY FOCUS ON MY HOMEWORK. BRING UP MY GRADES SO I DON'T HEAR "SEE ME AFTER CLASS" ANYMORE.
I GOTCHA. WELL, WE'RE GOING ROLLER SKATING THIS WEEKEND, AFTER THE BASEBALL GAME. SEE YOU THERE?
YEAH, MAYBE...
LATER.
YOUR TEACHER CALLED. WHAT'S THE MATTER, VIOLET? SHE SAID YOU WERE SLEEPING IN CLASS. THAT'S NOT LIKE YOU!
I DON'T KNOW, MOM. I GUESS... IT ALL SEEMS SO BORING AND POINTLESS.
ALL THE OTHER KIDS ARE INTERESTED IN CLOTHES, CARS, MOVIES... THEY'RE WORRYING ABOUT GEOMETRY WHILE THERE ARE MAD SCIENTISTS OUT THERE BUILDING DEATH RAYS!
EXCEPT FOR YOU GUYS, I CAN'T TALK TO ANYONE ABOUT THAT STUFF.
I GET IT NOW. THIS HAPPENS TO ALL OF US, VIOLET. THAT'S WHY IT'S IMPORTANT TO MAINTAIN A HEALTHY SUPER/CIVILIAN BALANCE.
YOUR SECRET IDENTITY IS AS IMPORTANT AS YOUR SUPER IDENTITY. IT'S WHAT KEEPS YOU GROUNDED.

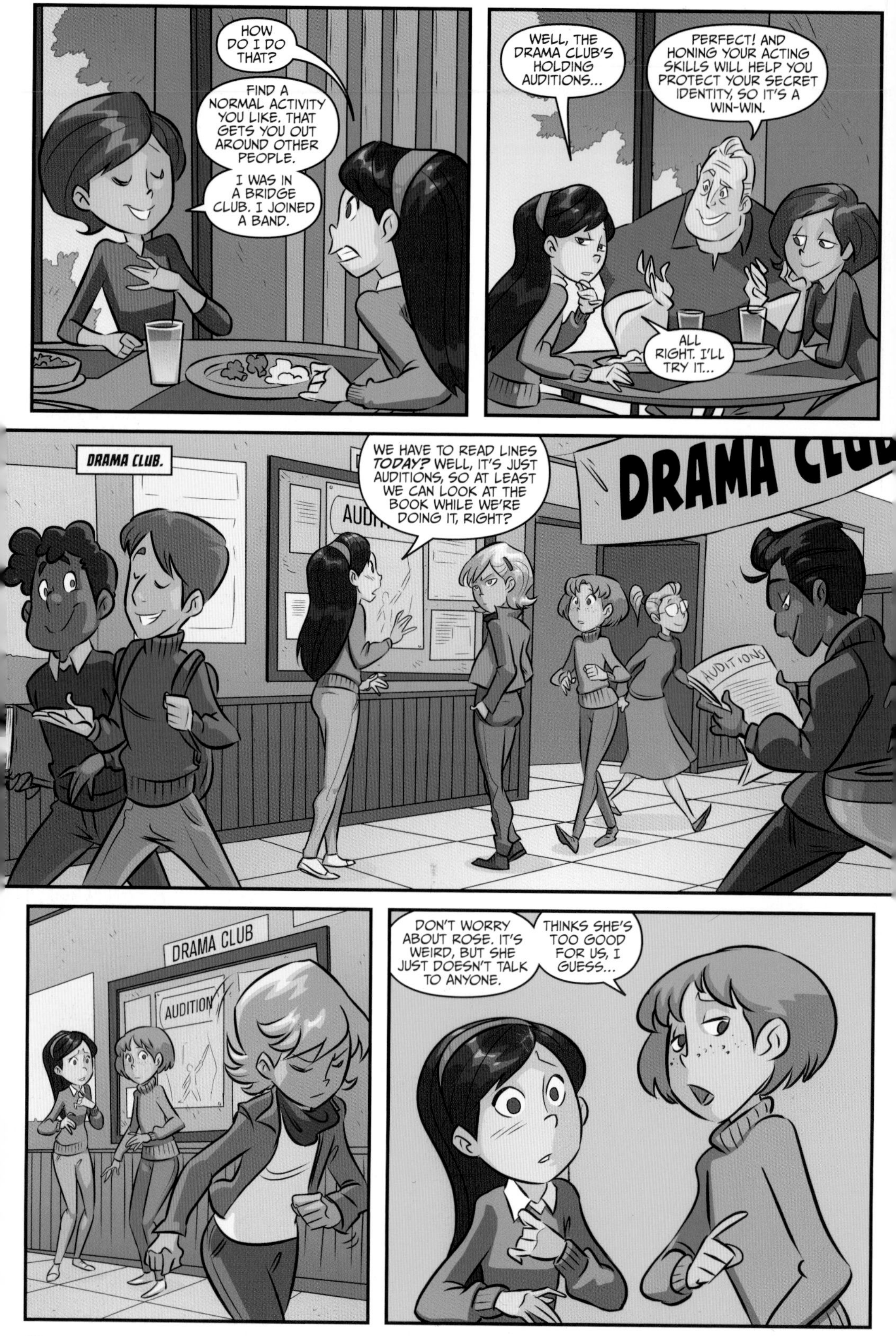
HOW DO I DO THAT?
FIND A NORMAL ACTIVITY YOU LIKE. THAT GETS YOU OUT AROUND OTHER PEOPLE.
I WAS IN A BRIDGE CLUB. I JOINED A BAND.
WELL, THE DRAMA CLUB'S HOLDING AUDITIONS...
PERFECT! AND HONING YOUR ACTING SKILLS WILL HELP YOU PROTECT YOUR SECRET IDENTITY, SO IT'S A WIN-WIN.
ALL RIGHT. I'LL TRY IT...
DRAMA CLUB.
WE HAVE TO READ LINES *TODAY?* WELL, IT'S JUST AUDITIONS, SO AT LEAST WE CAN LOOK AT THE BOOK WHILE WE'RE DOING IT, RIGHT?
DRAMA CLUB
AUDITIONS
DRAMA CLUB
AUDITION
DON'T WORRY ABOUT ROSE. IT'S WEIRD, BUT SHE JUST DOESN'T TALK TO ANYONE.
THINKS SHE'S TOO GOOD FOR US, I GUESS...

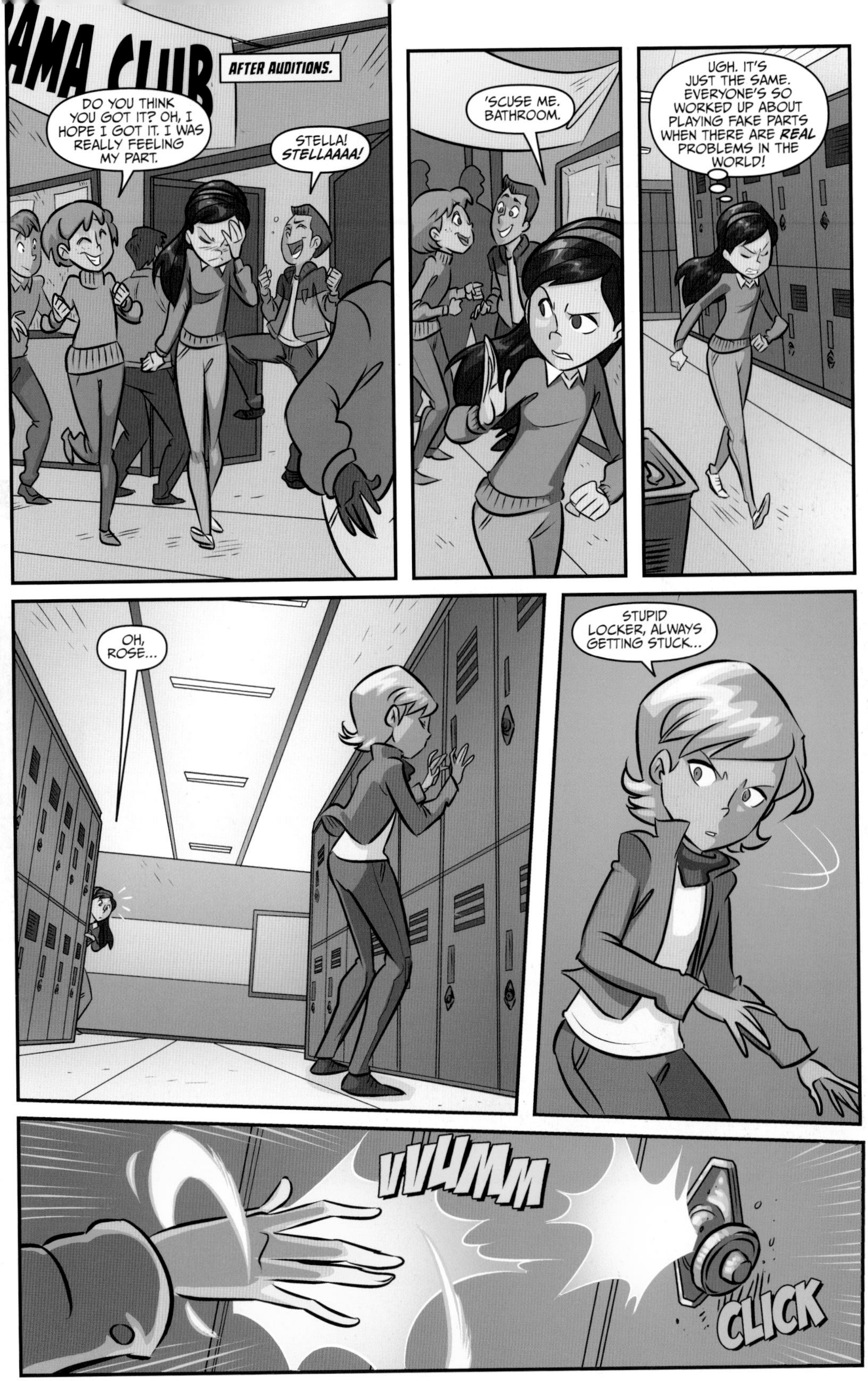
AMA CLUB
AFTER AUDITIONS.
DO YOU THINK YOU GOT IT? OH, I HOPE I GOT IT. I WAS REALLY FEELING MY PART.
STELLA! STELLAAAA!
'SCUSE ME. BATHROOM.
UGH. IT'S JUST THE SAME. EVERYONE'S SO WORKED UP ABOUT PLAYING FAKE PARTS WHEN THERE ARE REAL PROBLEMS IN THE WORLD!
OH, ROSE...
STUPID LOCKER, ALWAYS GETTING STUCK...
VVUMM
CLICK

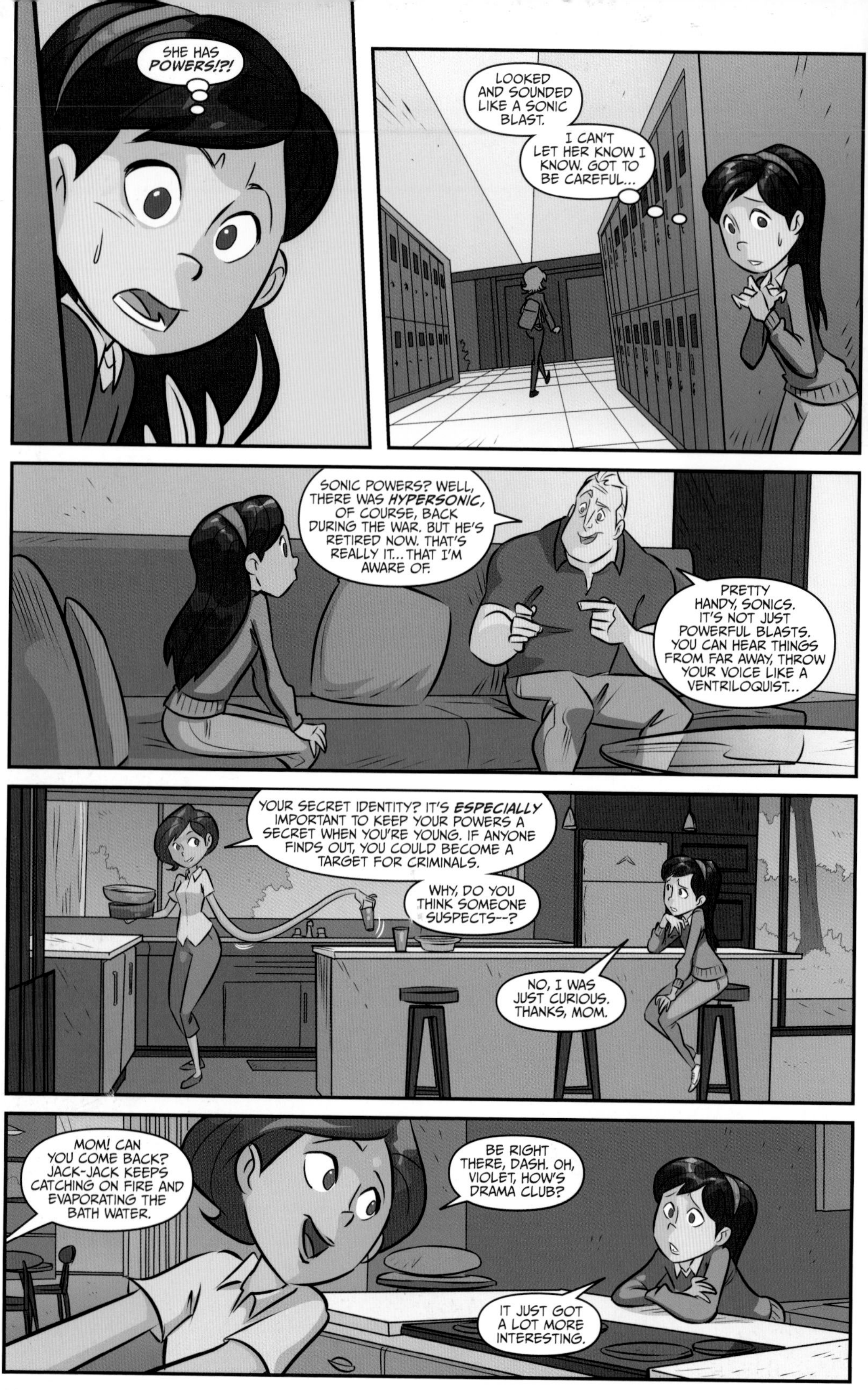
SHE HAS *POWERS!?!*
LOOKED AND SOUNDED LIKE A SONIC BLAST.
I CAN'T LET HER KNOW I KNOW. GOT TO BE CAREFUL...
SONIC POWERS? WELL, THERE WAS *HYPERSONIC*, OF COURSE, BACK DURING THE WAR. BUT HE'S RETIRED NOW. THAT'S REALLY IT... THAT I'M AWARE OF.
PRETTY HANDY, SONICS. IT'S NOT JUST POWERFUL BLASTS. YOU CAN HEAR THINGS FROM FAR AWAY, THROW YOUR VOICE LIKE A VENTRILOQUIST...
YOUR SECRET IDENTITY? IT'S *ESPECIALLY* IMPORTANT TO KEEP YOUR POWERS A SECRET WHEN YOU'RE YOUNG. IF ANYONE FINDS OUT, YOU COULD BECOME A TARGET FOR CRIMINALS.
WHY, DO YOU THINK SOMEONE SUSPECTS--?
NO, I WAS JUST CURIOUS. THANKS, MOM.
MOM! CAN YOU COME BACK? JACK-JACK KEEPS CATCHING ON FIRE AND EVAPORATING THE BATH WATER.
BE RIGHT THERE, DASH. OH, VIOLET, HOW'S DRAMA CLUB?
IT JUST GOT A LOT MORE INTERESTING.

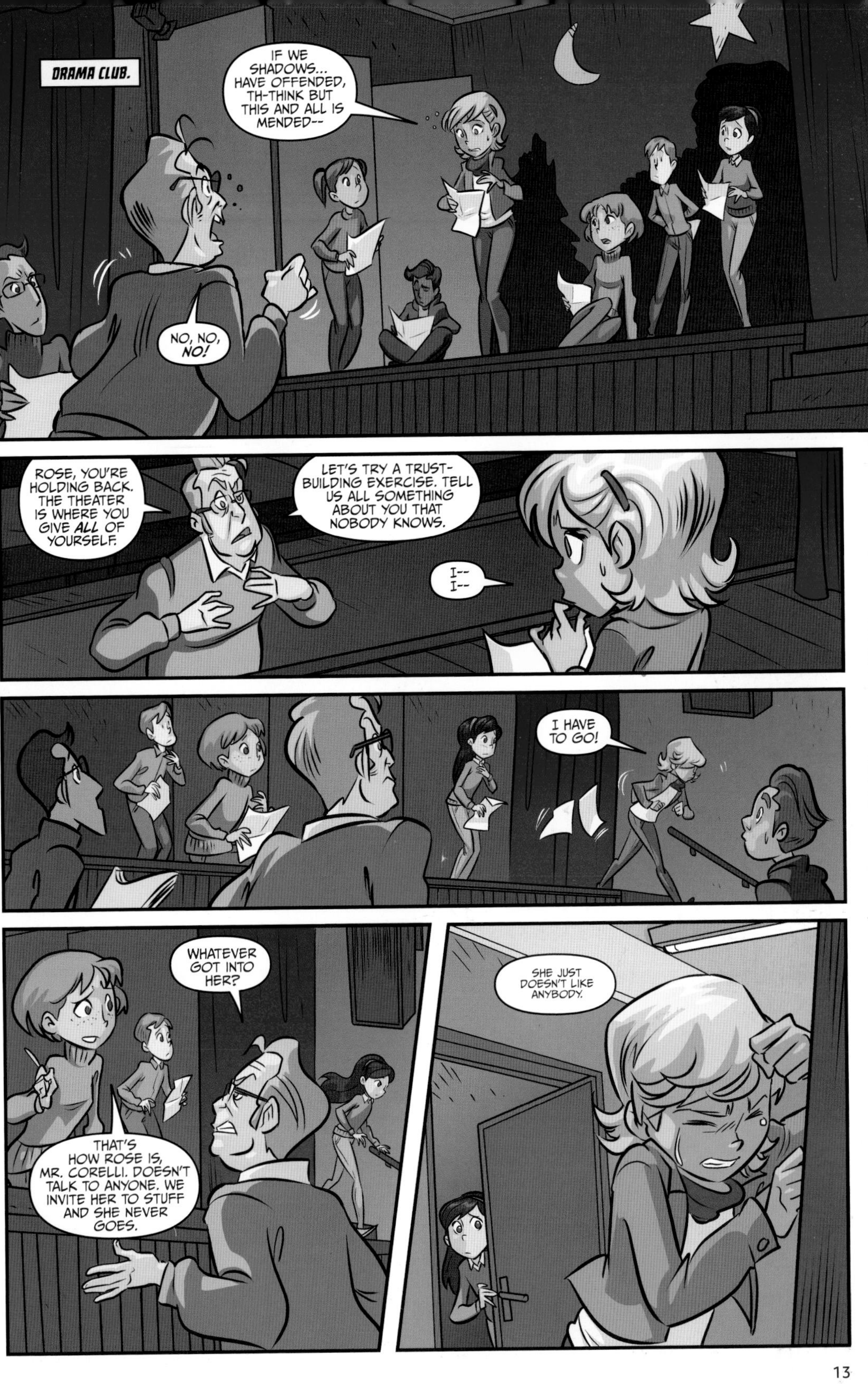
DRAMA CLUB.
IF WE SHADOWS... HAVE OFFENDED, TH-THINK BUT THIS AND ALL IS MENDED--
NO, NO, NO!
ROSE, YOU'RE HOLDING BACK. THE THEATER IS WHERE YOU GIVE ALL OF YOURSELF.
LET'S TRY A TRUST-BUILDING EXERCISE. TELL US ALL SOMETHING ABOUT YOU THAT NOBODY KNOWS.
I-- I--
I HAVE TO GO!
WHATEVER GOT INTO HER?
THAT'S HOW ROSE IS, MR. CORELLI. DOESN'T TALK TO ANYONE. WE INVITE HER TO STUFF AND SHE NEVER GOES.
SHE JUST DOESN'T LIKE ANYBODY.

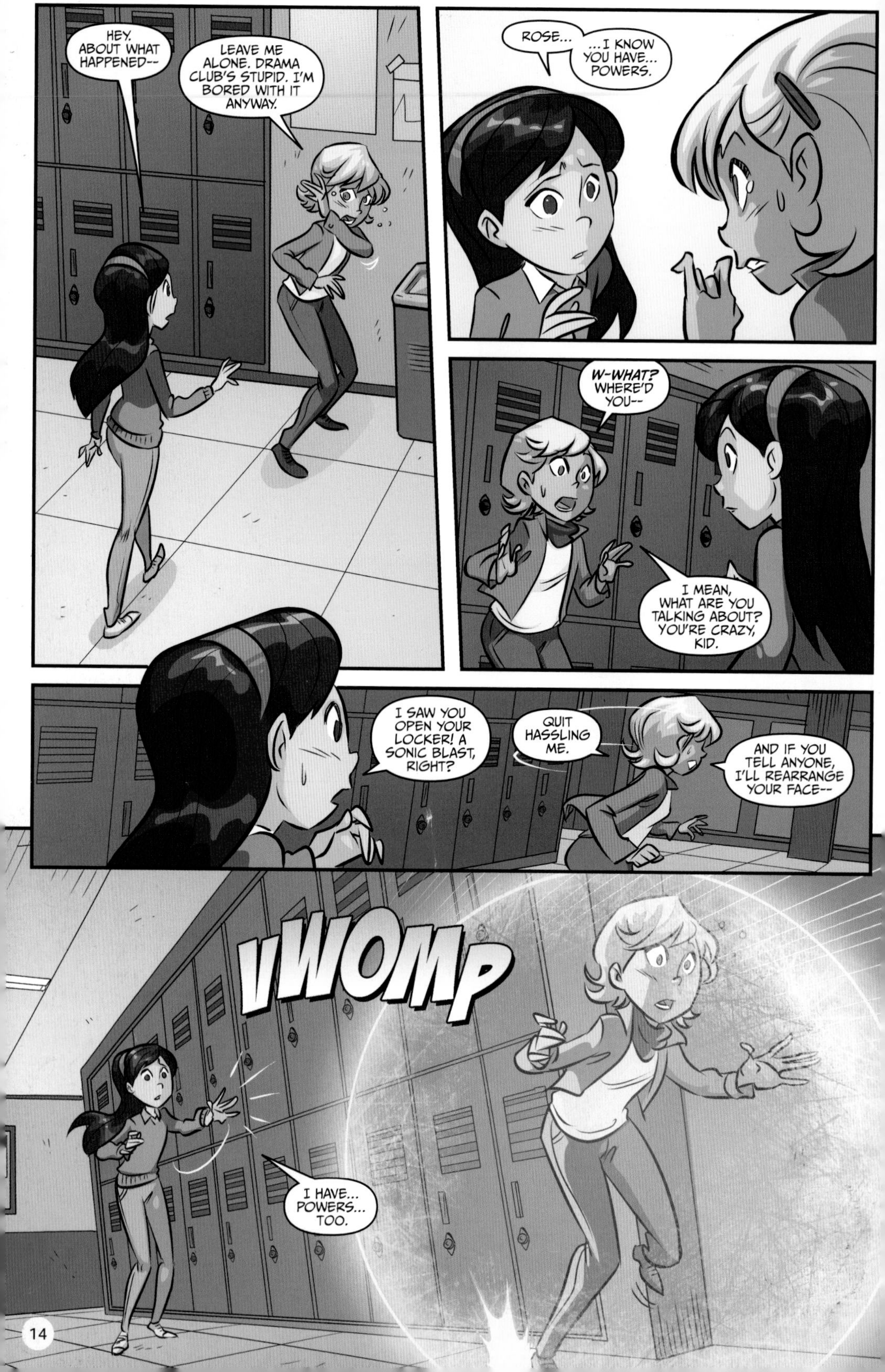
HEY. ABOUT WHAT HAPPENED--
LEAVE ME ALONE. DRAMA CLUB'S STUPID. I'M BORED WITH IT ANYWAY.
ROSE...
...I KNOW YOU HAVE... POWERS.
W-WHAT? WHERE'D YOU--
I MEAN, WHAT ARE YOU TALKING ABOUT? YOU'RE CRAZY, KID.
I SAW YOU OPEN YOUR LOCKER! A SONIC BLAST, RIGHT?
QUIT HASSLING ME.
AND IF YOU TELL ANYONE, I'LL REARRANGE YOUR FACE--
VWOMP
I HAVE... POWERS... TOO.

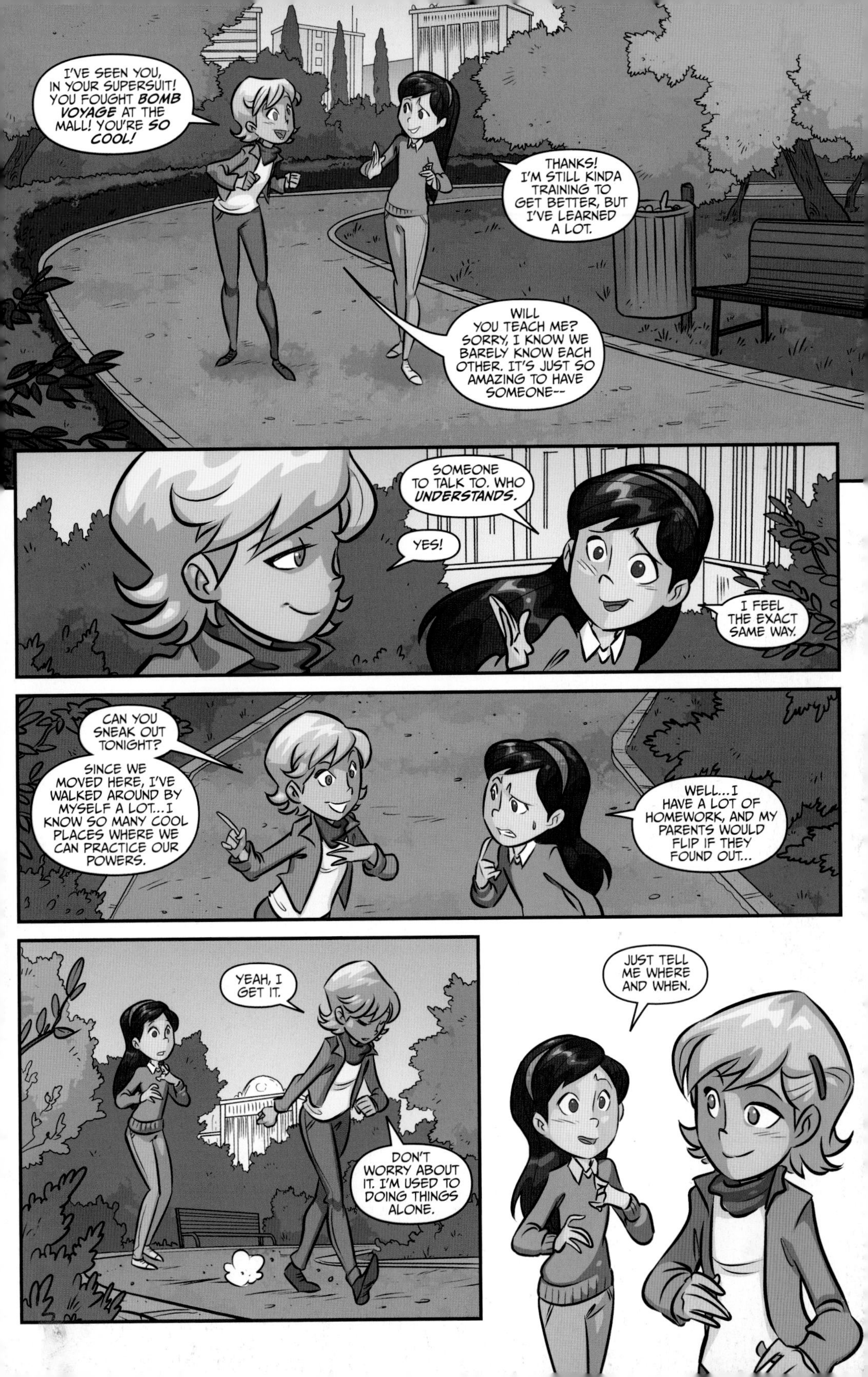
I'VE SEEN YOU, IN YOUR SUPERSUIT! YOU FOUGHT **BOMB VOYAGE** AT THE MALL! YOU'RE **SO COOL!**
THANKS! I'M STILL KINDA TRAINING TO GET BETTER, BUT I'VE LEARNED A LOT.
WILL YOU TEACH ME? SORRY, I KNOW WE BARELY KNOW EACH OTHER. IT'S JUST SO AMAZING TO HAVE SOMEONE--
SOMEONE TO TALK TO. WHO ***UNDERSTANDS.***
YES!
I FEEL THE EXACT SAME WAY.
CAN YOU SNEAK OUT TONIGHT?
SINCE WE MOVED HERE, I'VE WALKED AROUND BY MYSELF A LOT...I KNOW SO MANY COOL PLACES WHERE WE CAN PRACTICE OUR POWERS.
WELL...I HAVE A LOT OF HOMEWORK, AND MY PARENTS WOULD FLIP IF THEY FOUND OUT...
YEAH, I GET IT.
DON'T WORRY ABOUT IT. I'M USED TO DOING THINGS ALONE.
JUST TELL ME WHERE AND WHEN.

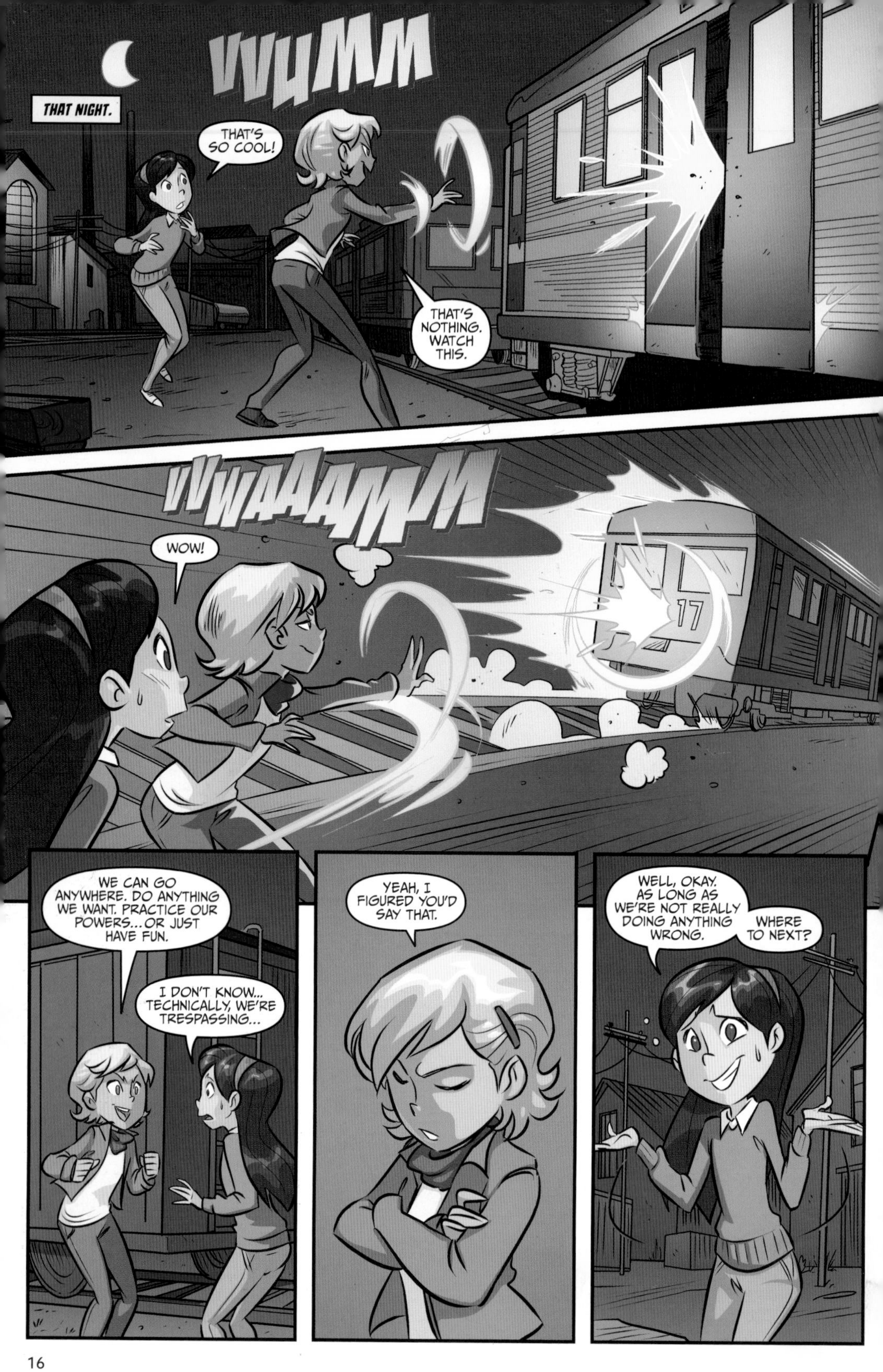
VVUMM
THAT NIGHT.
THAT'S SO COOL!
THAT'S NOTHING. WATCH THIS.
VVWAAAMM
WOW!
17
WE CAN GO ANYWHERE. DO ANYTHING WE WANT. PRACTICE OUR POWERS...OR JUST HAVE FUN.
I DON'T KNOW... TECHNICALLY, WE'RE TRESPASSING...
YEAH, I FIGURED YOU'D SAY THAT.
WELL, OKAY. AS LONG AS WE'RE NOT REALLY DOING ANYTHING WRONG.
WHERE TO NEXT?

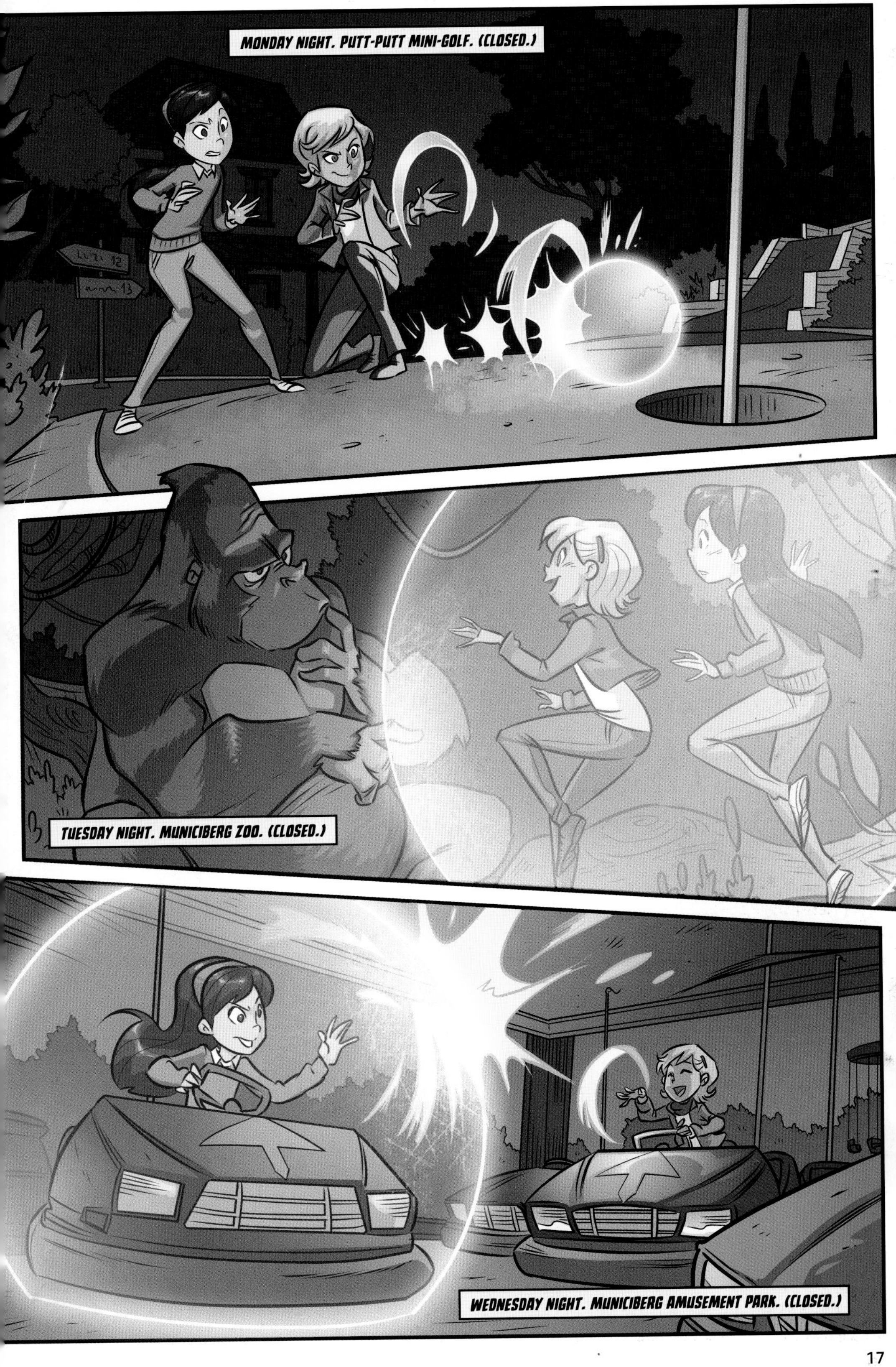
MONDAY NIGHT. PUTT-PUTT MINI-GOLF. (CLOSED.)
TUESDAY NIGHT. MUNICIBERG ZOO. (CLOSED.)
WEDNESDAY NIGHT. MUNICIBERG AMUSEMENT PARK. (CLOSED.)

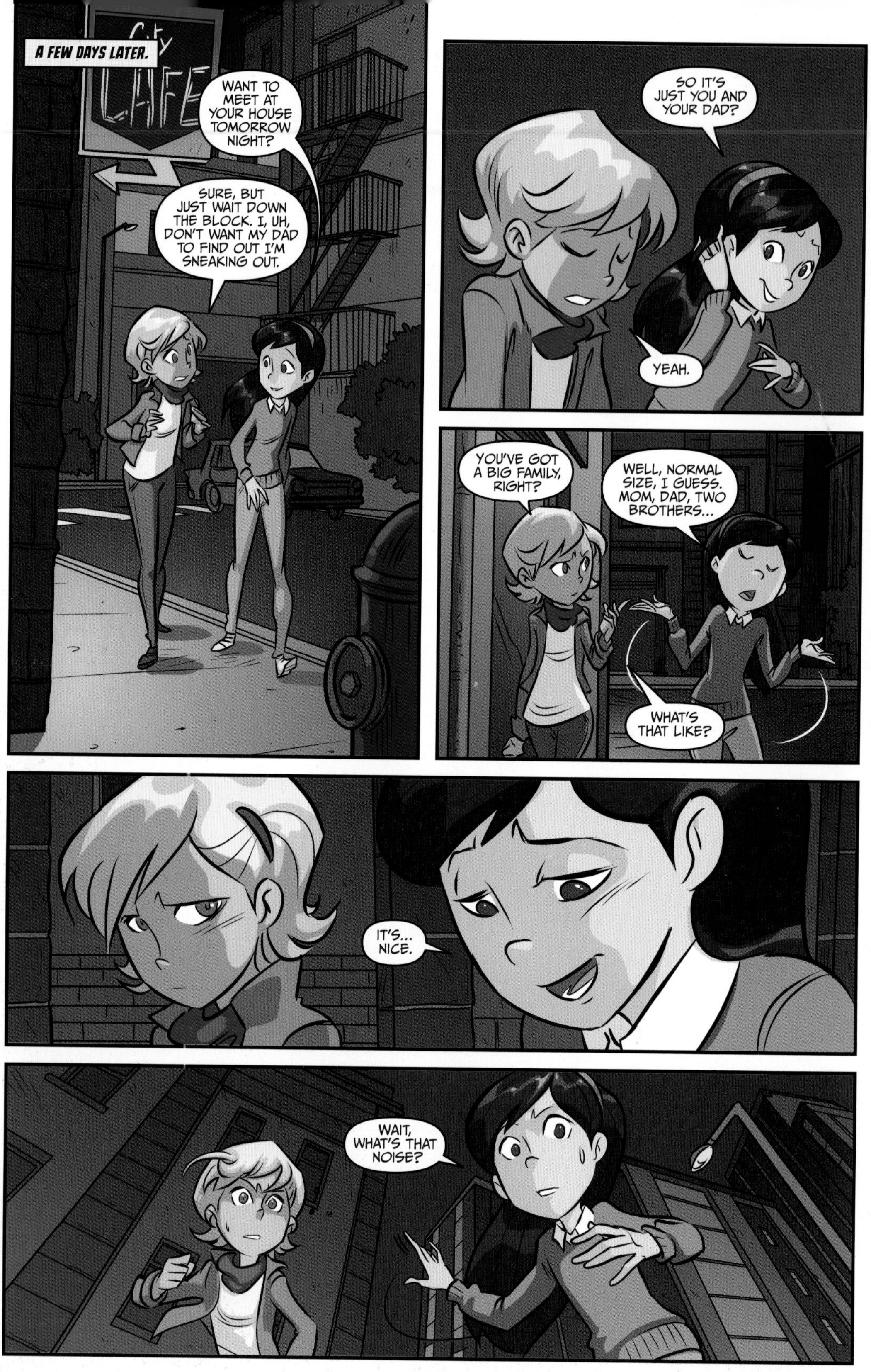
A FEW DAYS LATER.
CITY CAFE
WANT TO MEET AT YOUR HOUSE TOMORROW NIGHT?
SURE, BUT JUST WAIT DOWN THE BLOCK. I, UH, DON'T WANT MY DAD TO FIND OUT I'M SNEAKING OUT.
SO IT'S JUST YOU AND YOUR DAD?
YEAH.
YOU'VE GOT A BIG FAMILY, RIGHT?
WELL, NORMAL SIZE, I GUESS. MOM, DAD, TWO BROTHERS...
WHAT'S THAT LIKE?
IT'S... NICE.
WAIT, WHAT'S THAT NOISE?

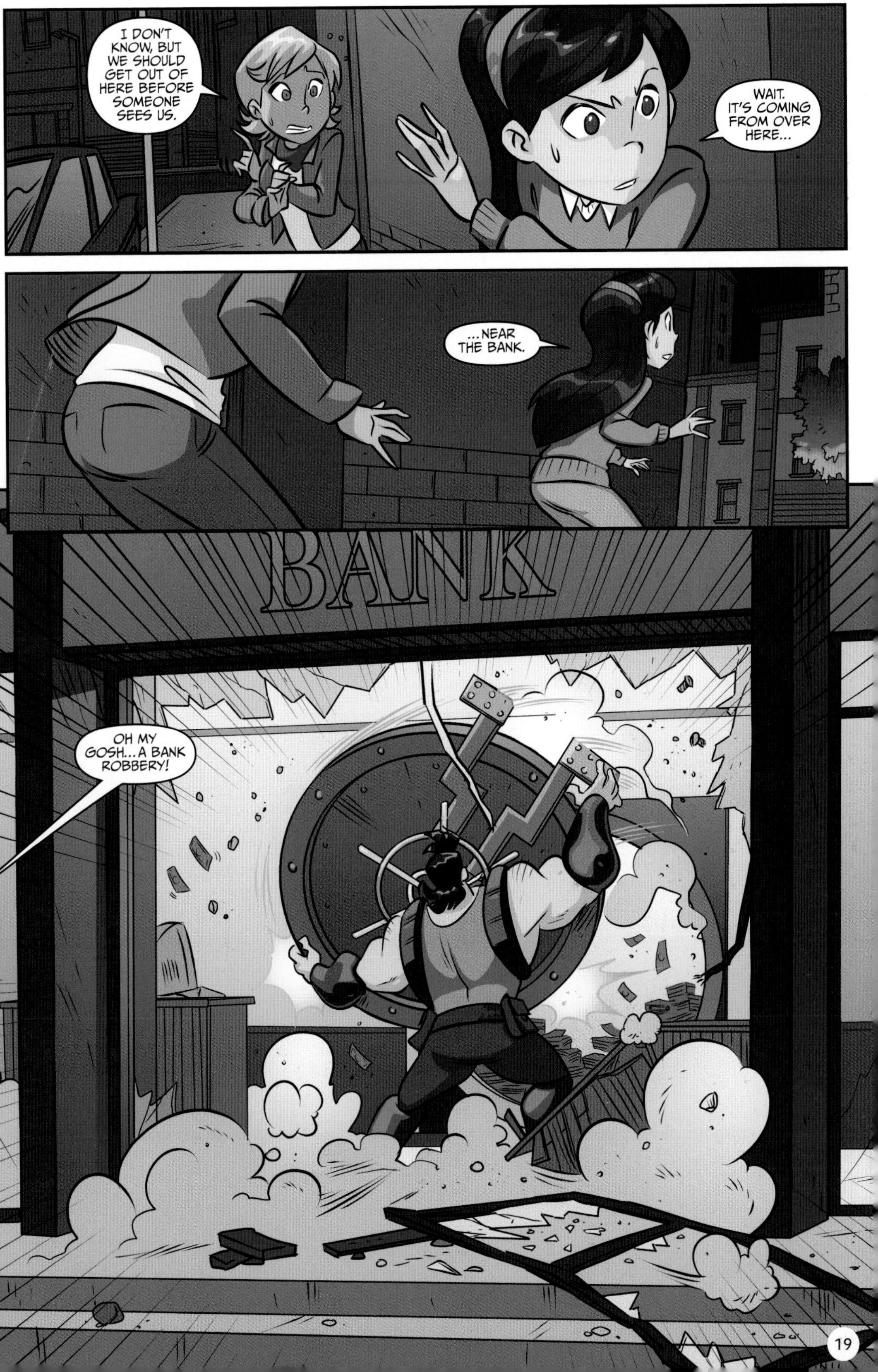
I DON'T KNOW, BUT WE SHOULD GET OUT OF HERE BEFORE SOMEONE SEES US.
WAIT. IT'S COMING FROM OVER HERE...
...NEAR THE BANK.
BANK
OH MY GOSH...A BANK ROBBERY!

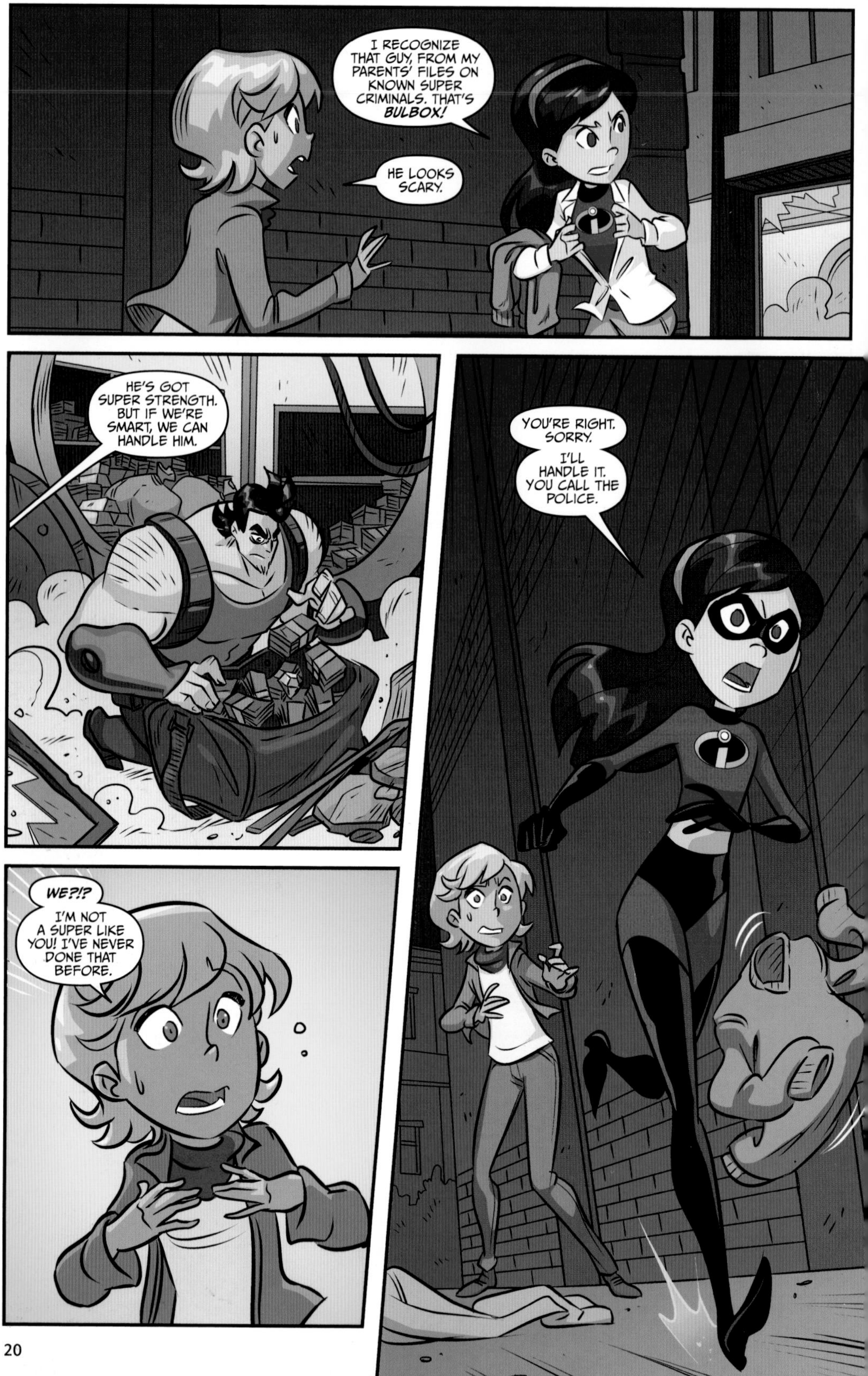
I RECOGNIZE THAT GUY, FROM MY PARENTS' FILES ON KNOWN SUPER CRIMINALS. THAT'S *BULBOX!*
HE LOOKS SCARY.
HE'S GOT SUPER STRENGTH. BUT IF WE'RE SMART, WE CAN HANDLE HIM.
WE?!?
I'M NOT A SUPER LIKE YOU! I'VE NEVER DONE THAT BEFORE.
YOU'RE RIGHT. SORRY.
I'LL HANDLE IT. YOU CALL THE POLICE.

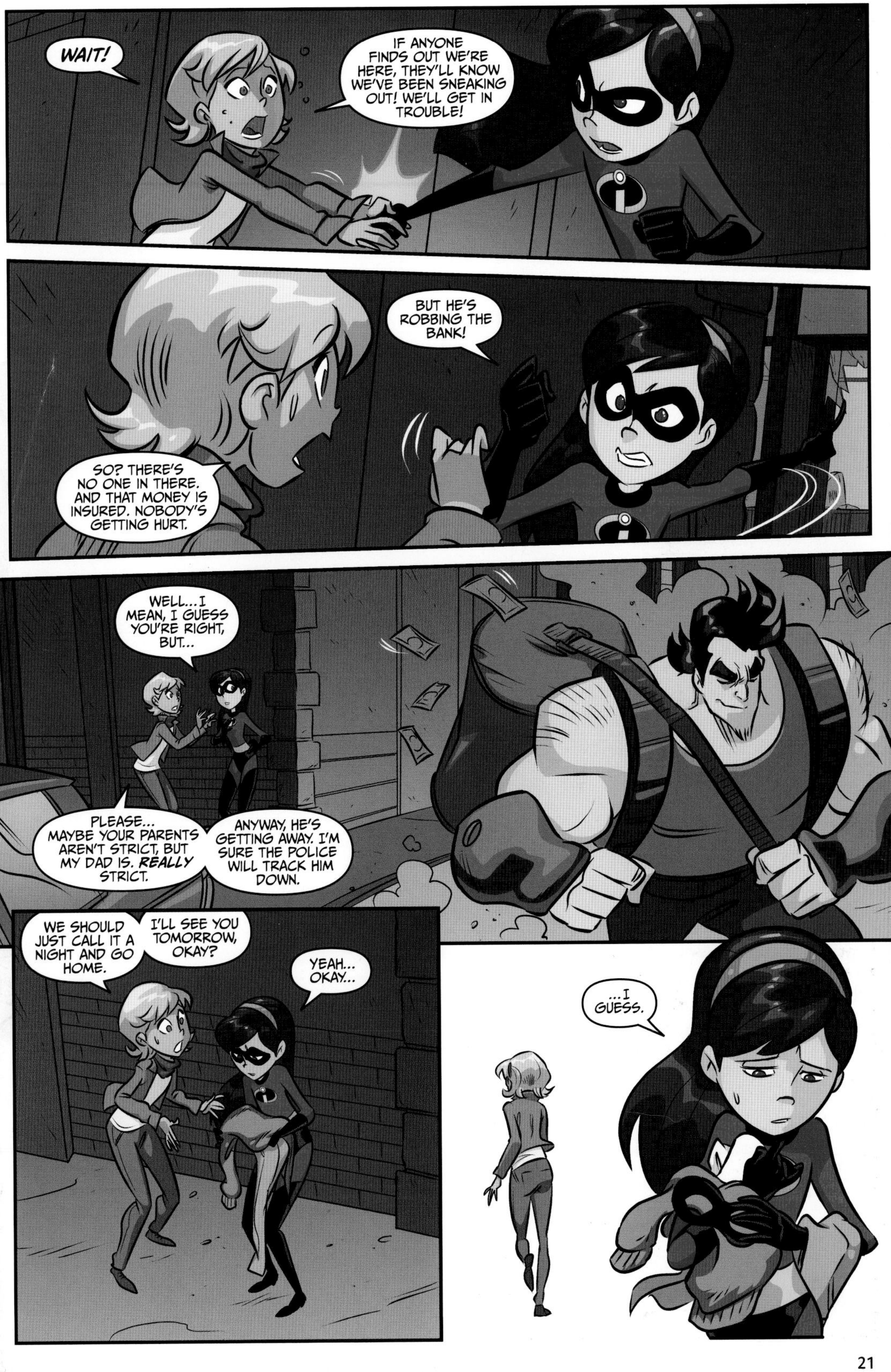
WAIT!
IF ANYONE FINDS OUT WE'RE HERE, THEY'LL KNOW WE'VE BEEN SNEAKING OUT! WE'LL GET IN TROUBLE!
BUT HE'S ROBBING THE BANK!
SO? THERE'S NO ONE IN THERE. AND THAT MONEY IS INSURED. NOBODY'S GETTING HURT.
WELL... I MEAN, I GUESS YOU'RE RIGHT, BUT...
PLEASE... MAYBE YOUR PARENTS AREN'T STRICT, BUT MY DAD IS. *REALLY* STRICT.
ANYWAY, HE'S GETTING AWAY. I'M SURE THE POLICE WILL TRACK HIM DOWN.
WE SHOULD JUST CALL IT A NIGHT AND GO HOME.
I'LL SEE YOU TOMORROW, OKAY?
YEAH... OKAY...
...I GUESS.

THE NEXT DAY.

I THINK MAYBE WE SHOULD'VE DONE SOMETHING LAST NIGHT.

SHH! YOU WANT TO GET US IN TROUBLE?

ANYWAY, IT'S TOO LATE NOW. THE BEST THING TO DO IS FORGET ABOUT IT.

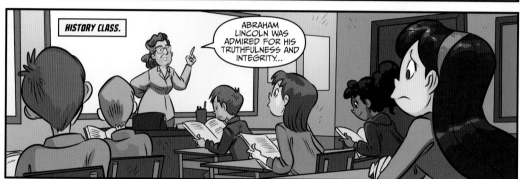

HISTORY CLASS.

ABRAHAM LINCOLN WAS ADMIRED FOR HIS TRUTHFULNESS AND INTEGRITY...

LUNCH.

PRINCIPAL LELAND, SOMEONE DROPPED THEIR WALLET.

THANKS, VIOLET. I'LL SEE THEY GET IT BACK. YOU'RE ALWAYS SO HONEST.

UH... YEAH.

DRAMA CLUB.

SUSPICION ALWAYS HAUNTS THE GUILTY MIND...

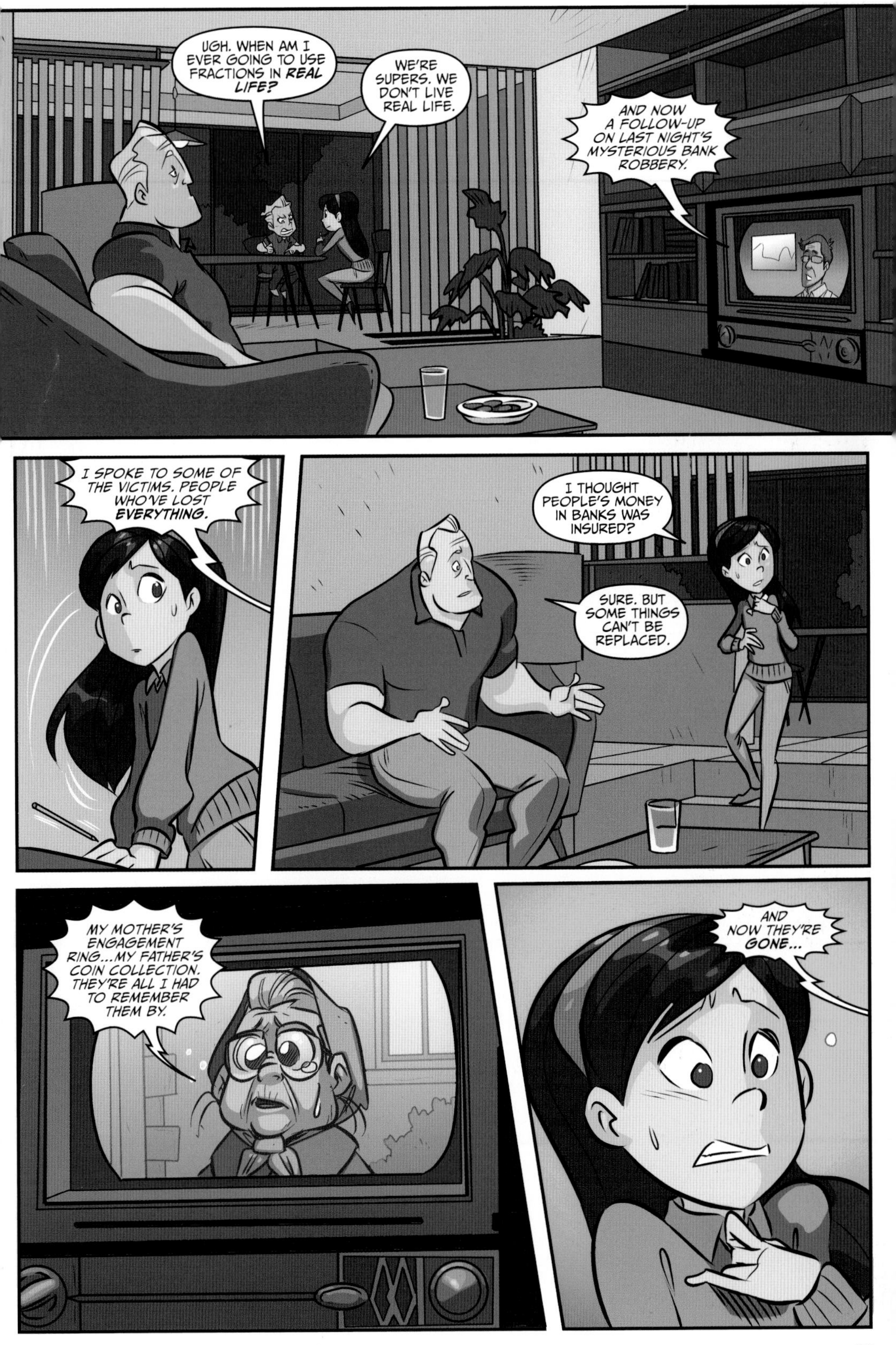
UGH. WHEN AM I EVER GOING TO USE FRACTIONS IN **REAL LIFE?**
WE'RE SUPERS. WE DON'T LIVE REAL LIFE.
AND NOW A FOLLOW-UP ON LAST NIGHT'S MYSTERIOUS BANK ROBBERY.
I SPOKE TO SOME OF THE VICTIMS. PEOPLE WHO'VE LOST **EVERYTHING.**
I THOUGHT PEOPLE'S MONEY IN BANKS WAS INSURED?
SURE. BUT SOME THINGS CAN'T BE REPLACED.
MY MOTHER'S ENGAGEMENT RING...MY FATHER'S COIN COLLECTION. THEY'RE ALL I HAD TO REMEMBER THEM BY.
AND NOW THEY'RE **GONE...**

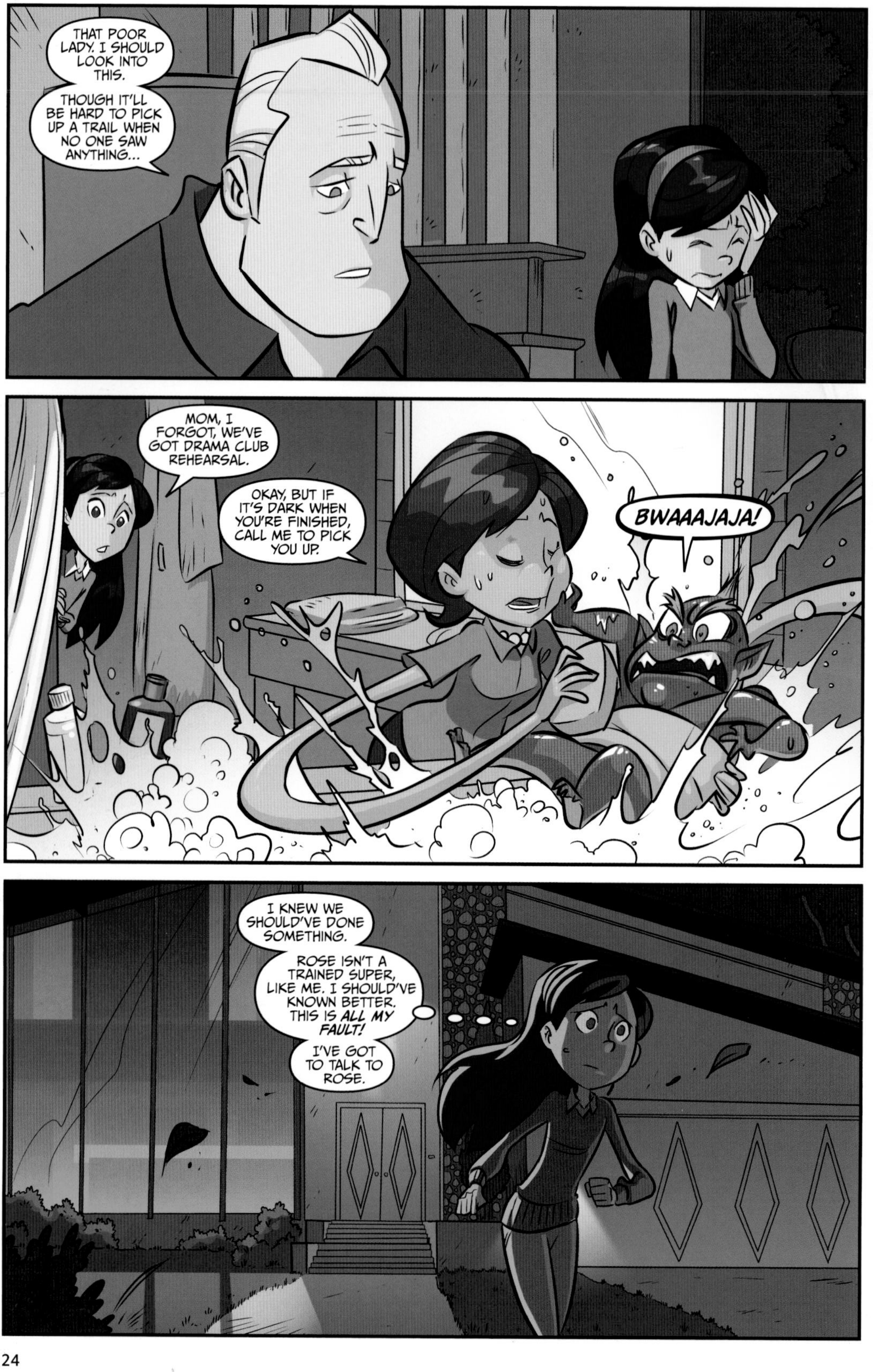
THAT POOR LADY. I SHOULD LOOK INTO THIS.
THOUGH IT'LL BE HARD TO PICK UP A TRAIL WHEN NO ONE SAW ANYTHING...
MOM, I FORGOT, WE'VE GOT DRAMA CLUB REHEARSAL.
OKAY, BUT IF IT'S DARK WHEN YOU'RE FINISHED, CALL ME TO PICK YOU UP.
BWAAAJAJA!
I KNEW WE SHOULD'VE DONE SOMETHING.
ROSE ISN'T A TRAINED SUPER, LIKE ME. I SHOULD'VE KNOWN BETTER. THIS IS ALL MY FAULT!
I'VE GOT TO TALK TO ROSE.

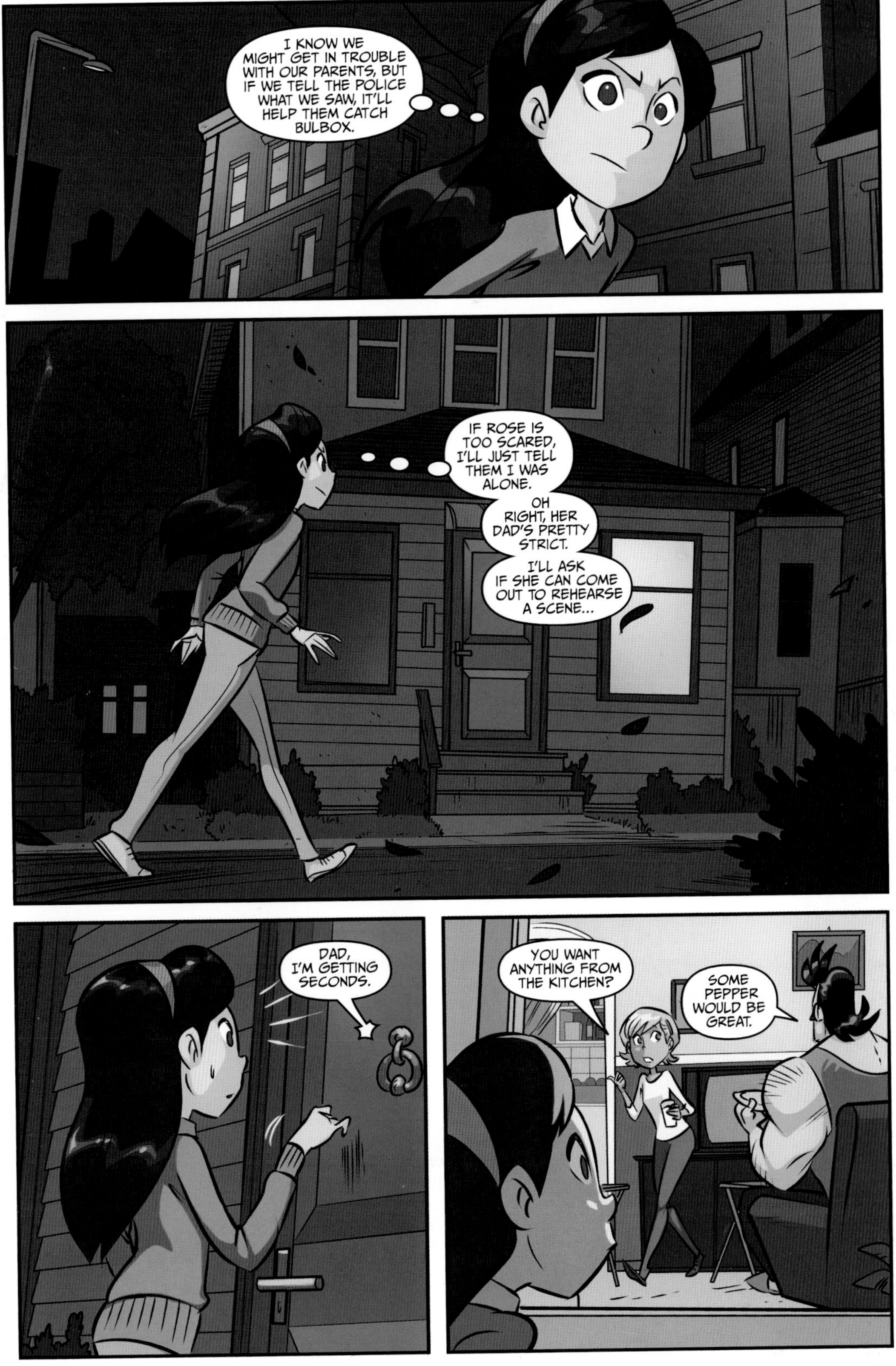
I KNOW WE MIGHT GET IN TROUBLE WITH OUR PARENTS, BUT IF WE TELL THE POLICE WHAT WE SAW, IT'LL HELP THEM CATCH BULBOX.
IF ROSE IS TOO SCARED, I'LL JUST TELL THEM I WAS ALONE.
OH RIGHT, HER DAD'S PRETTY STRICT.
I'LL ASK IF SHE CAN COME OUT TO REHEARSE A SCENE...
DAD, I'M GETTING SECONDS.
YOU WANT ANYTHING FROM THE KITCHEN?
SOME PEPPER WOULD BE GREAT.

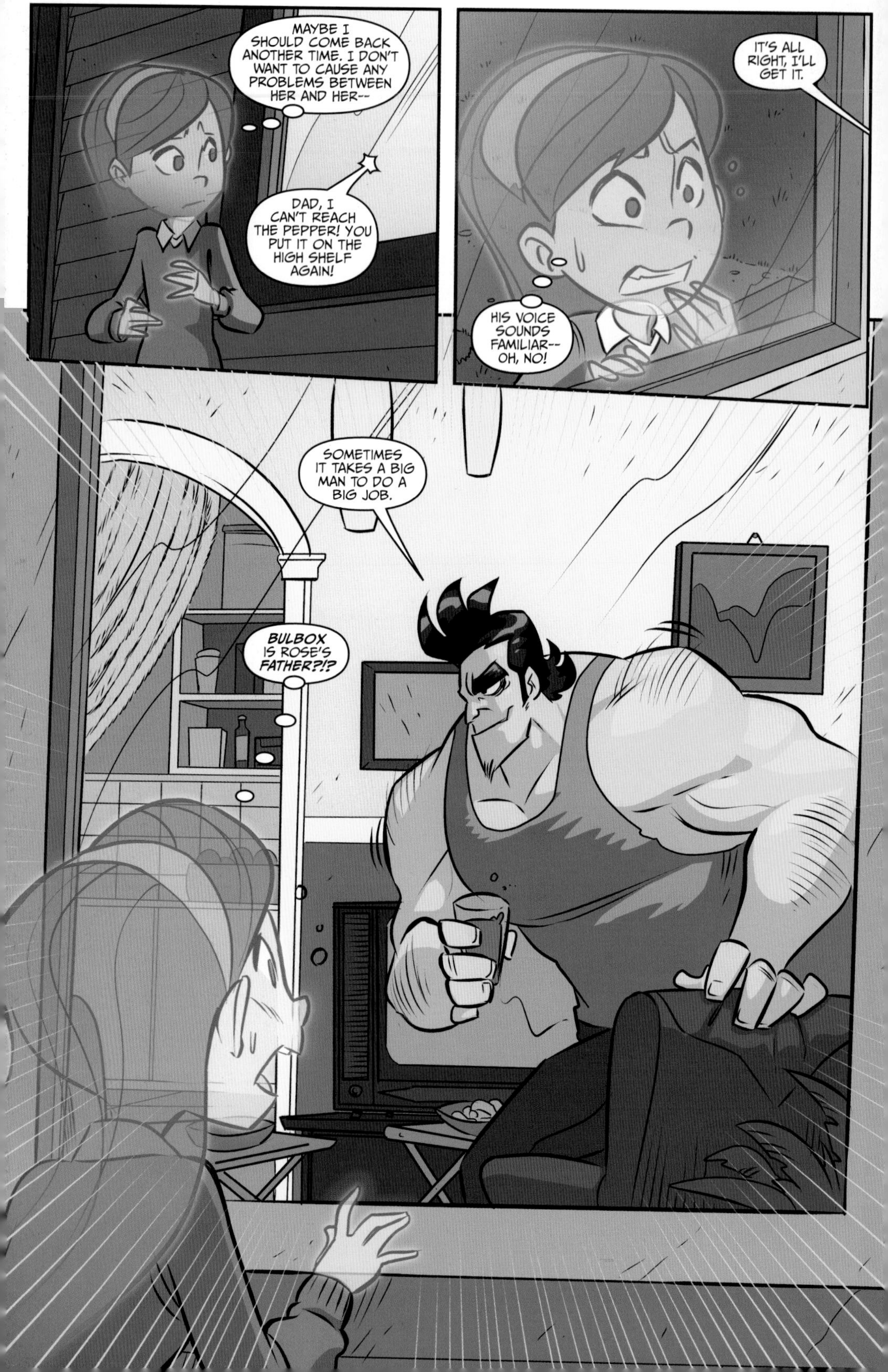
MAYBE I SHOULD COME BACK ANOTHER TIME. I DON'T WANT TO CAUSE ANY PROBLEMS BETWEEN HER AND HER--
DAD, I CAN'T REACH THE PEPPER! YOU PUT IT ON THE HIGH SHELF AGAIN!
IT'S ALL RIGHT, I'LL GET IT.
HIS VOICE SOUNDS FAMILIAR-- OH, NO!
SOMETIMES IT TAKES A BIG MAN TO DO A BIG JOB.
BULBOX IS ROSE'S FATHER?!?

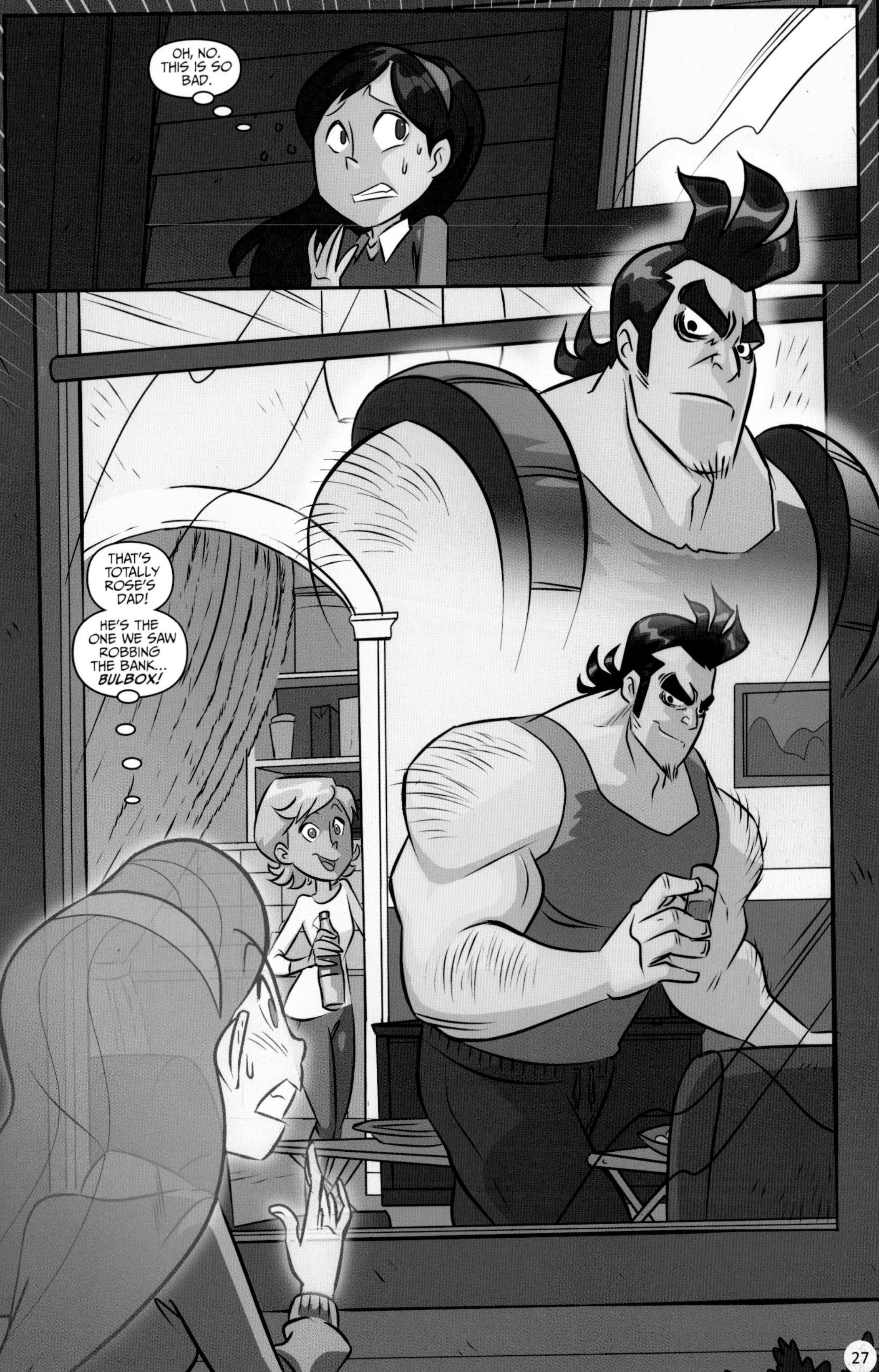
OH, NO. THIS IS SO BAD.
THAT'S TOTALLY ROSE'S DAD!
HE'S THE ONE WE SAW ROBBING THE BANK... **BULBOX!**

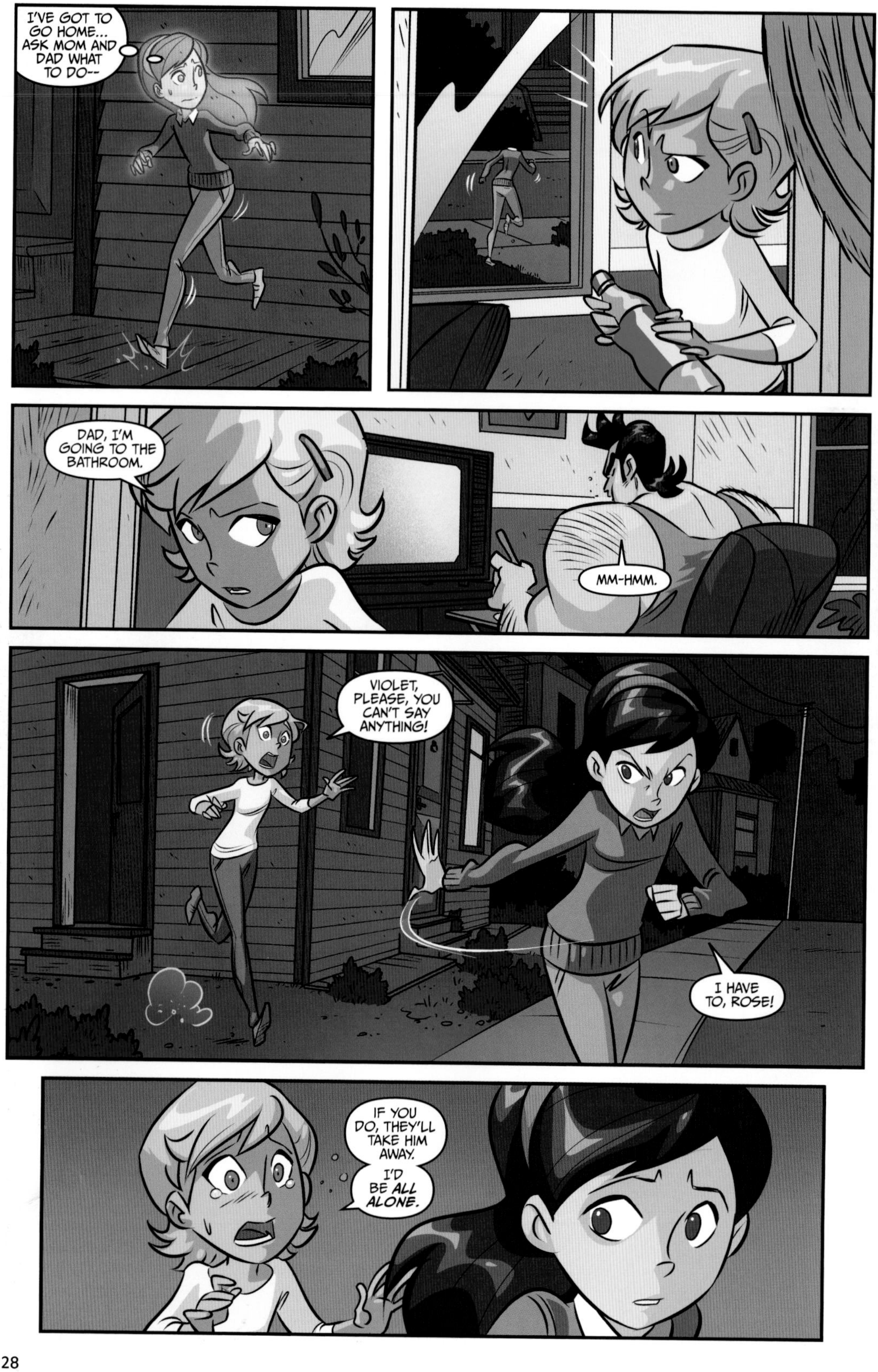
I'VE GOT TO GO HOME... ASK MOM AND DAD WHAT TO DO--
DAD, I'M GOING TO THE BATHROOM.
MM-HMM.
VIOLET, PLEASE, YOU CAN'T SAY ANYTHING!
I HAVE TO, ROSE!
IF YOU DO, THEY'LL TAKE HIM AWAY.
I'D BE ***ALL ALONE.***

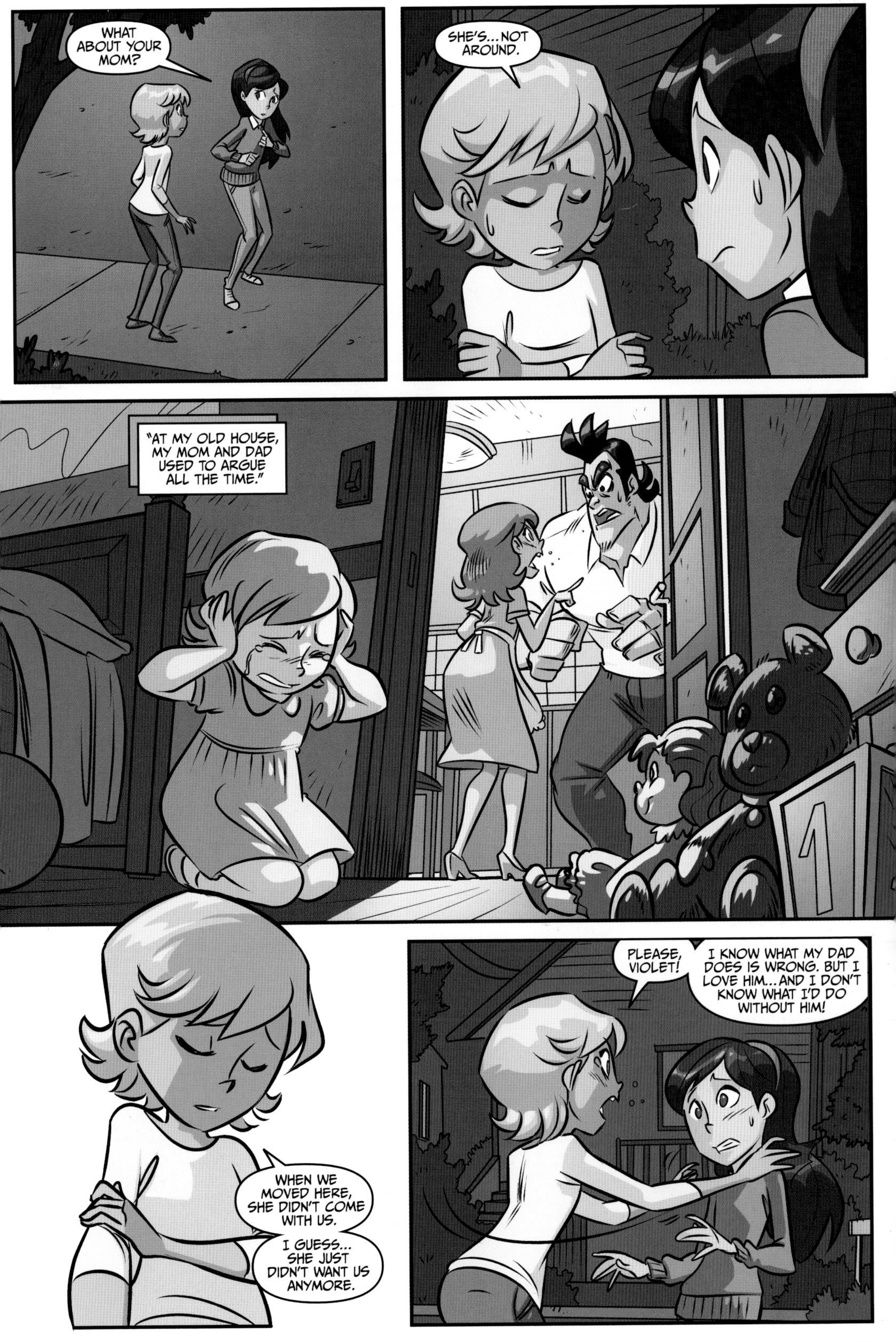
WHAT ABOUT YOUR MOM?
SHE'S...NOT AROUND.
"AT MY OLD HOUSE, MY MOM AND DAD USED TO ARGUE ALL THE TIME."
WHEN WE MOVED HERE, SHE DIDN'T COME WITH US.
I GUESS... SHE JUST DIDN'T WANT US ANYMORE.
PLEASE, VIOLET!
I KNOW WHAT MY DAD DOES IS WRONG. BUT I LOVE HIM...AND I DON'T KNOW WHAT I'D DO WITHOUT HIM!

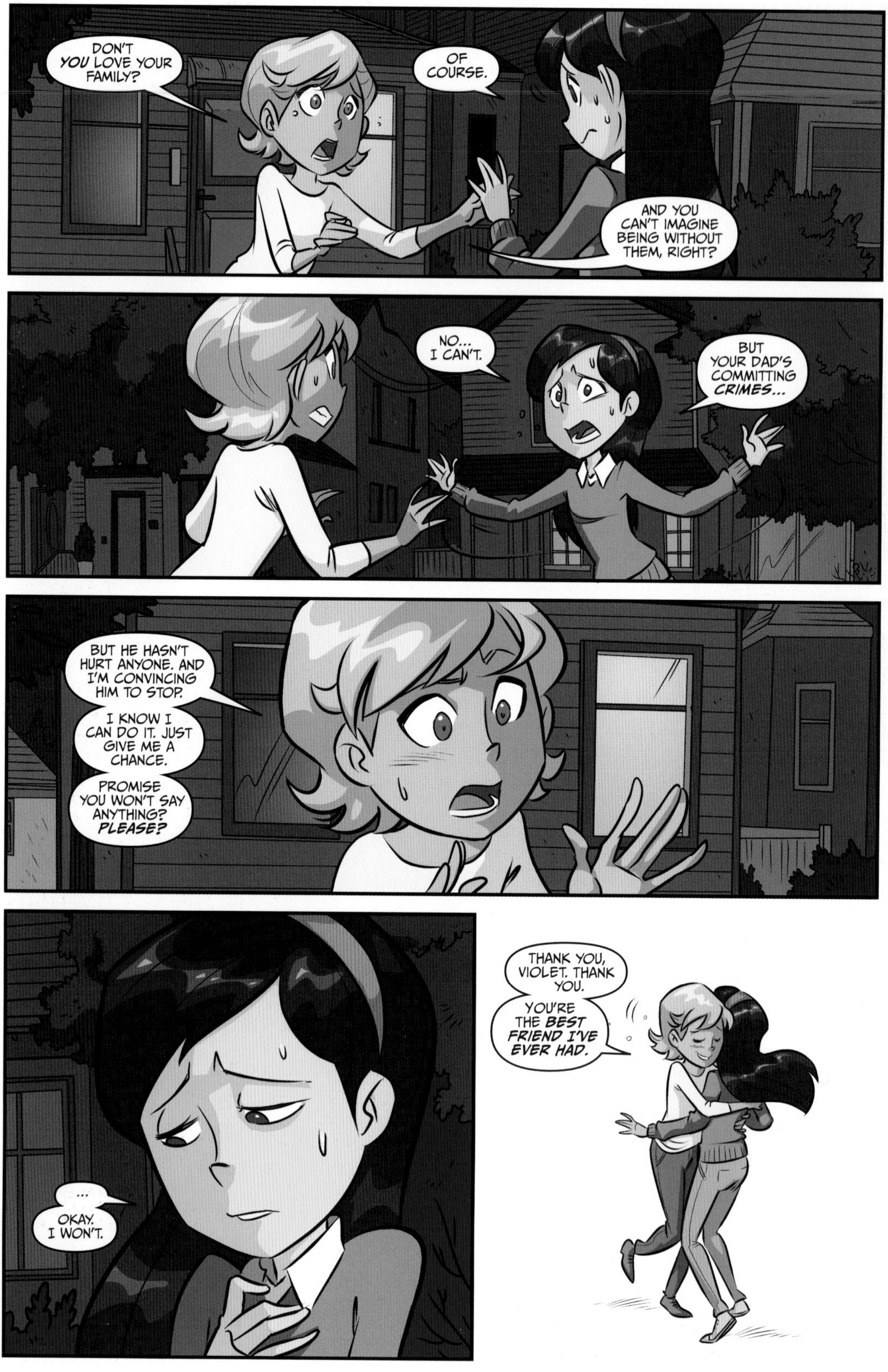
DON'T *YOU* LOVE YOUR FAMILY?
OF COURSE.
AND YOU CAN'T IMAGINE BEING WITHOUT THEM, RIGHT?
NO... I CAN'T.
BUT YOUR DAD'S COMMITTING *CRIMES...*
BUT HE HASN'T HURT ANYONE. AND I'M CONVINCING HIM TO STOP.
I KNOW I CAN DO IT. JUST GIVE ME A CHANCE.
PROMISE YOU WON'T SAY ANYTHING? *PLEASE?*
...
OKAY. I WON'T.
THANK YOU, VIOLET. THANK YOU.
YOU'RE THE *BEST FRIEND I'VE EVER HAD.*

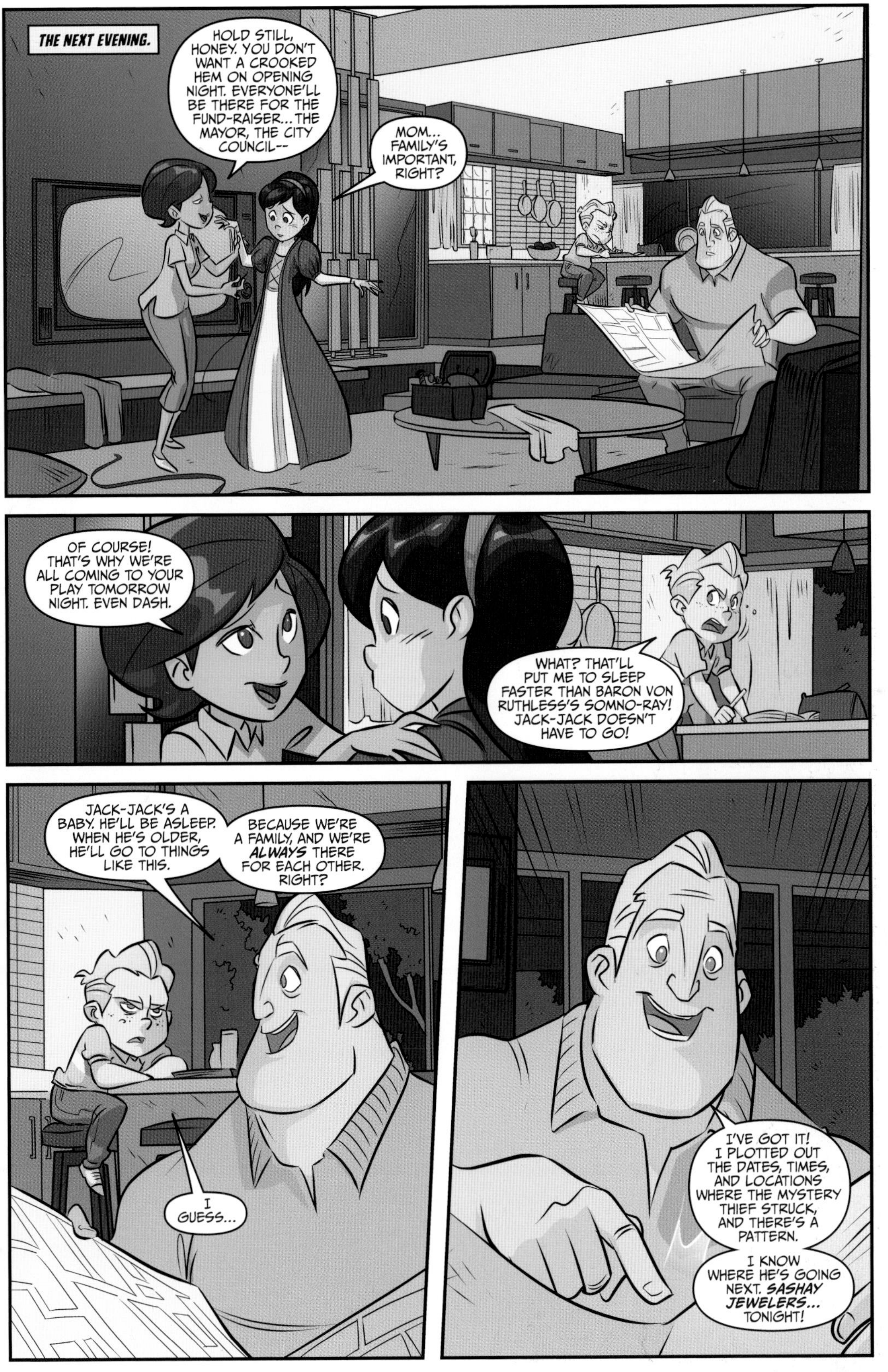
THE NEXT EVENING.
HOLD STILL, HONEY. YOU DON'T WANT A CROOKED HEM ON OPENING NIGHT. EVERYONE'LL BE THERE FOR THE FUND-RAISER... THE MAYOR, THE CITY COUNCIL--
MOM... FAMILY'S IMPORTANT, RIGHT?
OF COURSE! THAT'S WHY WE'RE ALL COMING TO YOUR PLAY TOMORROW NIGHT. EVEN DASH.
WHAT? THAT'LL PUT ME TO SLEEP FASTER THAN BARON VON RUTHLESS'S SOMNO-RAY! JACK-JACK DOESN'T HAVE TO GO!
JACK-JACK'S A BABY. HE'LL BE ASLEEP. WHEN HE'S OLDER, HE'LL GO TO THINGS LIKE THIS.
BECAUSE WE'RE A FAMILY, AND WE'RE ALWAYS THERE FOR EACH OTHER. RIGHT?
I GUESS...
I'VE GOT IT! I PLOTTED OUT THE DATES, TIMES, AND LOCATIONS WHERE THE MYSTERY THIEF STRUCK, AND THERE'S A PATTERN.
I KNOW WHERE HE'S GOING NEXT. SASHAY JEWELERS... TONIGHT!

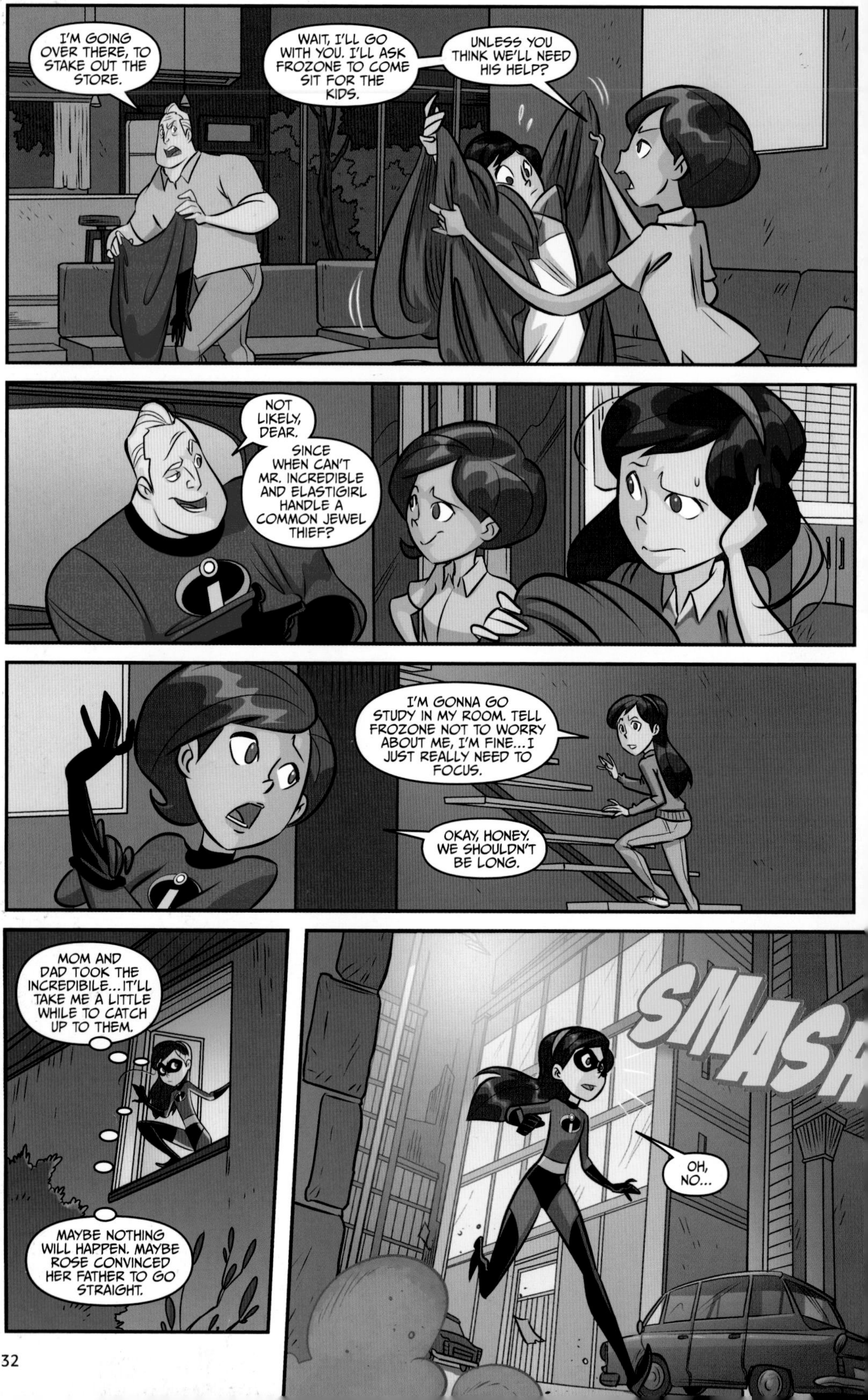
I'M GOING OVER THERE, TO STAKE OUT THE STORE.
WAIT, I'LL GO WITH YOU. I'LL ASK FROZONE TO COME SIT FOR THE KIDS.
UNLESS YOU THINK WE'LL NEED HIS HELP?
NOT LIKELY, DEAR.
SINCE WHEN CAN'T MR. INCREDIBLE AND ELASTIGIRL HANDLE A COMMON JEWEL THIEF?
I'M GONNA GO STUDY IN MY ROOM. TELL FROZONE NOT TO WORRY ABOUT ME, I'M FINE...I JUST REALLY NEED TO FOCUS.
OKAY, HONEY. WE SHOULDN'T BE LONG.
MOM AND DAD TOOK THE INCREDIBILE...IT'LL TAKE ME A LITTLE WHILE TO CATCH UP TO THEM.
MAYBE NOTHING WILL HAPPEN. MAYBE ROSE CONVINCED HER FATHER TO GO STRAIGHT.
SMASH
OH, NO...

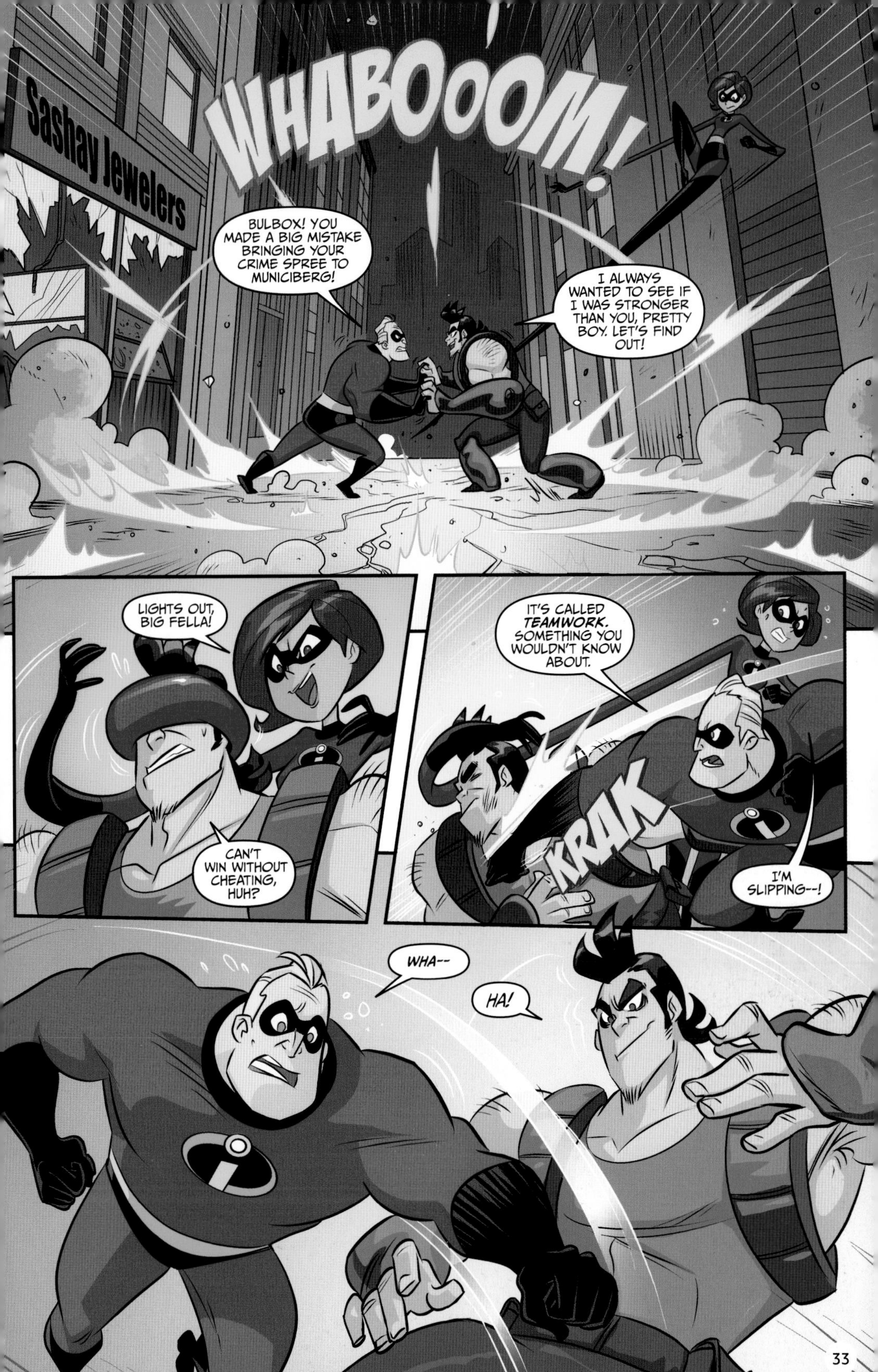

Sashay Jewelers
WHABOOOM!
BULBOX! YOU MADE A BIG MISTAKE BRINGING YOUR CRIME SPREE TO MUNICIBERG!
I ALWAYS WANTED TO SEE IF I WAS STRONGER THAN YOU, PRETTY BOY. LET'S FIND OUT!
LIGHTS OUT, BIG FELLA!
CAN'T WIN WITHOUT CHEATING, HUH?
IT'S CALLED **TEAMWORK.** SOMETHING YOU WOULDN'T KNOW ABOUT.
KRAK
I'M SLIPPING--!
WHA--
HA!

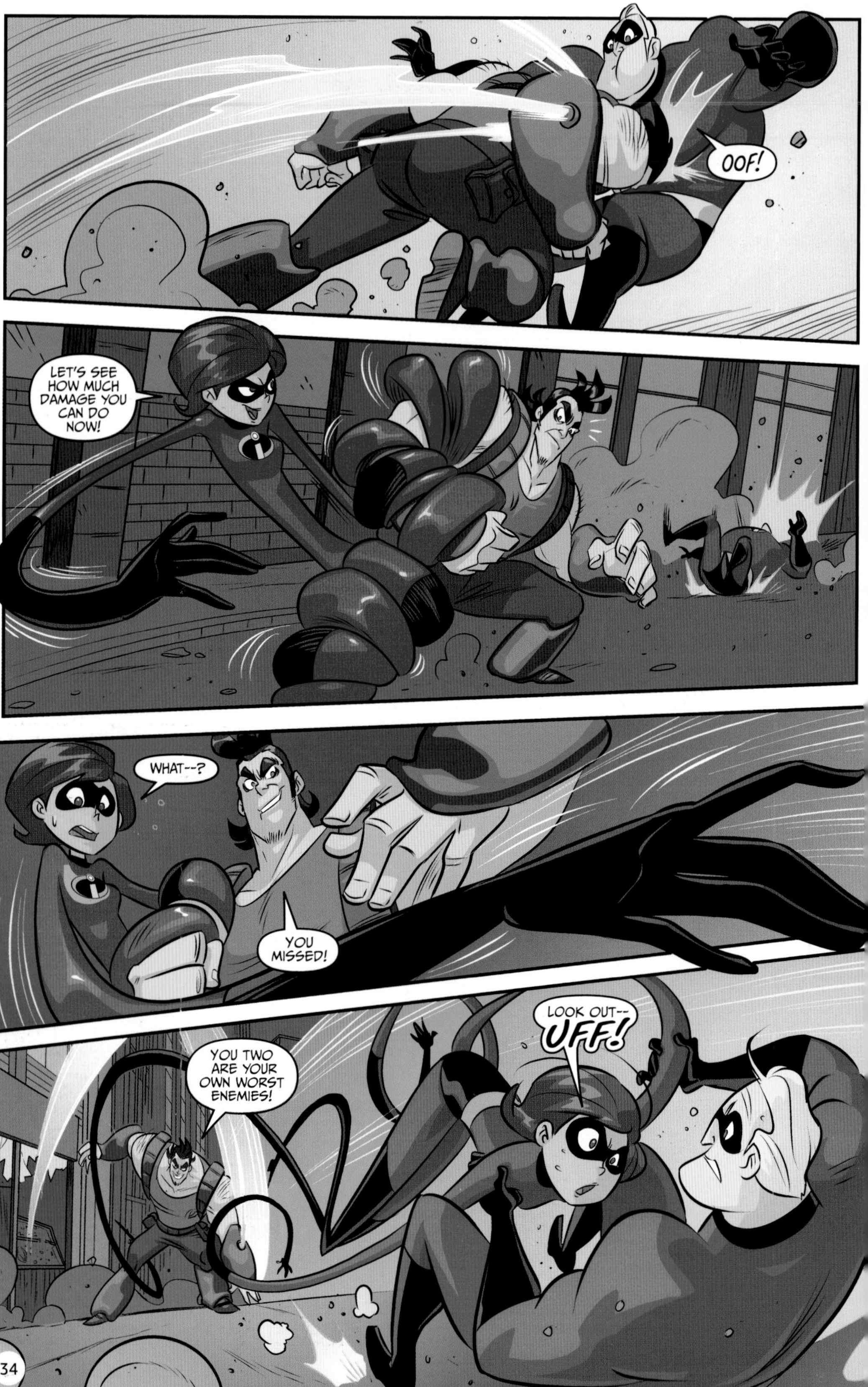
OOF!
LET'S SEE HOW MUCH DAMAGE YOU CAN DO NOW!
WHAT--?
YOU MISSED!
YOU TWO ARE YOUR OWN WORST ENEMIES!
LOOK OUT--
UFF!

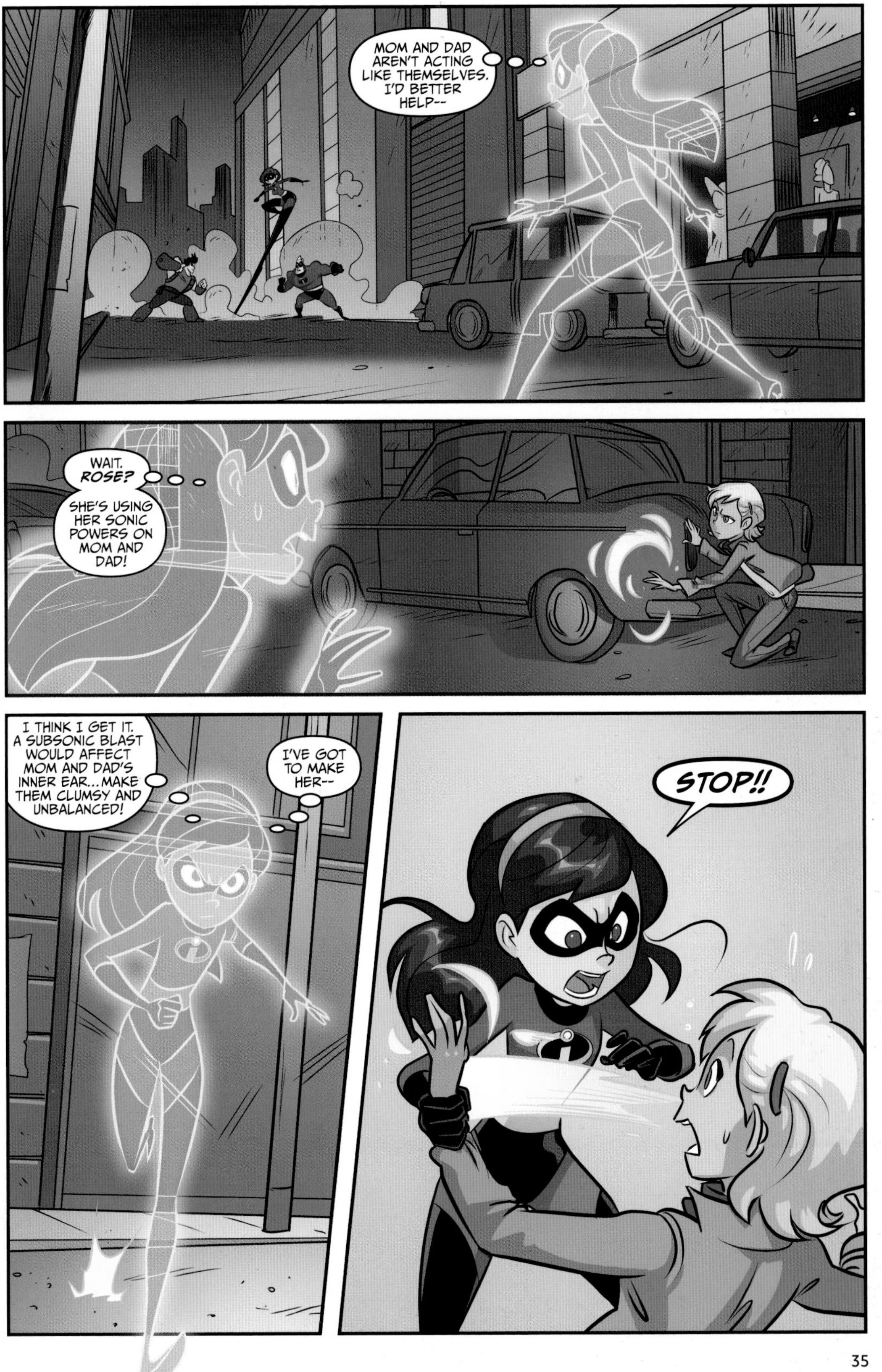
MOM AND DAD AREN'T ACTING LIKE THEMSELVES. I'D BETTER HELP--
WAIT. ROSE?
SHE'S USING HER SONIC POWERS ON MOM AND DAD!
I THINK I GET IT. A SUBSONIC BLAST WOULD AFFECT MOM AND DAD'S INNER EAR...MAKE THEM CLUMSY AND UNBALANCED!
I'VE GOT TO MAKE HER--
STOP!!

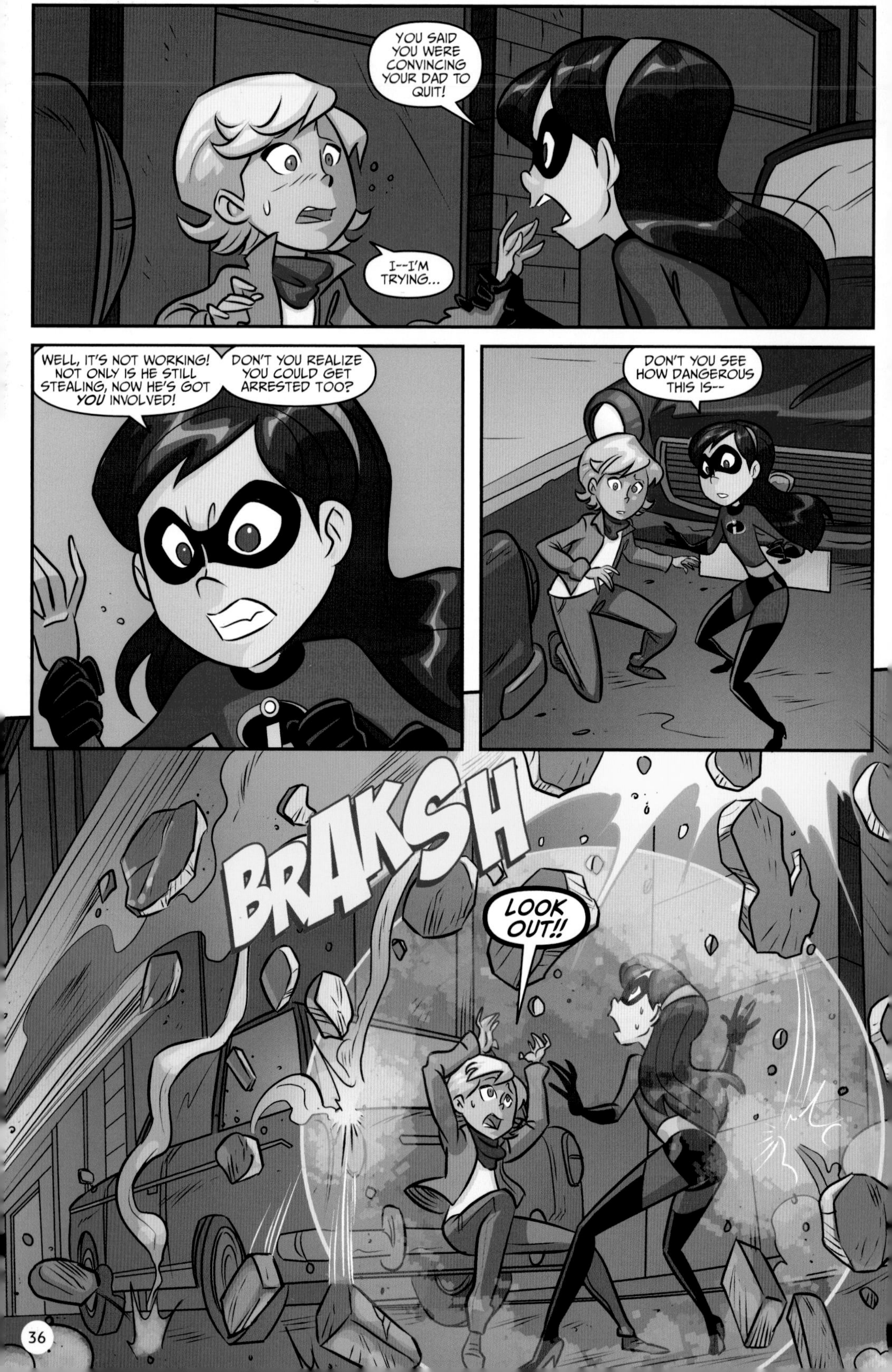

YOU SAID YOU WERE CONVINCING YOUR DAD TO QUIT!
I--I'M TRYING...
WELL, IT'S NOT WORKING! NOT ONLY IS HE STILL STEALING, NOW HE'S GOT *YOU* INVOLVED!
DON'T YOU REALIZE YOU COULD GET ARRESTED TOO?
DON'T YOU SEE HOW DANGEROUS THIS IS--
BRAKSH
LOOK OUT!!

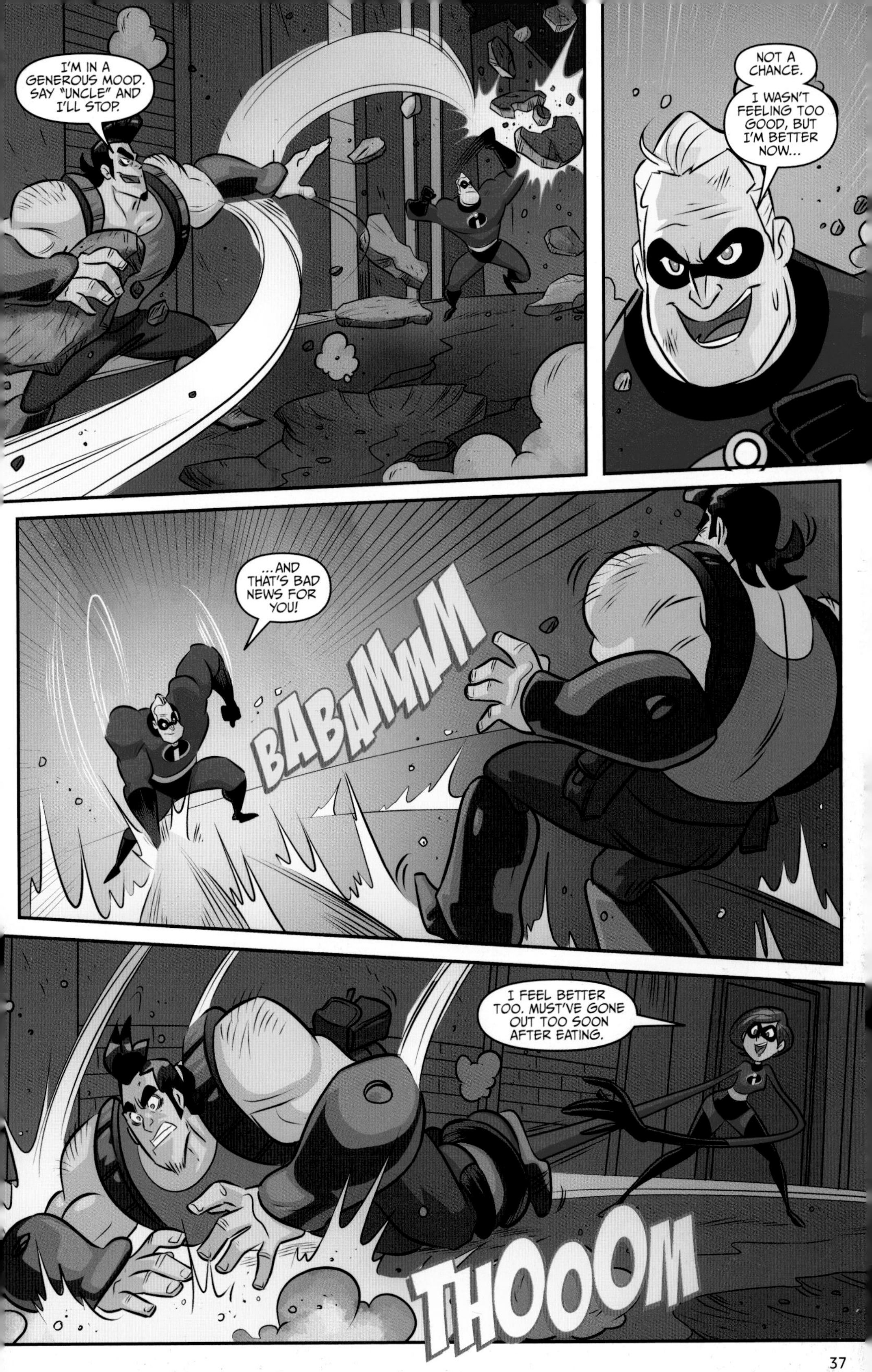
I'M IN A GENEROUS MOOD. SAY "UNCLE" AND I'LL STOP.
NOT A CHANCE.
I WASN'T FEELING TOO GOOD, BUT I'M BETTER NOW...
...AND THAT'S BAD NEWS FOR YOU!
BABAMMM
I FEEL BETTER TOO. MUST'VE GONE OUT TOO SOON AFTER EATING.
THOOOM

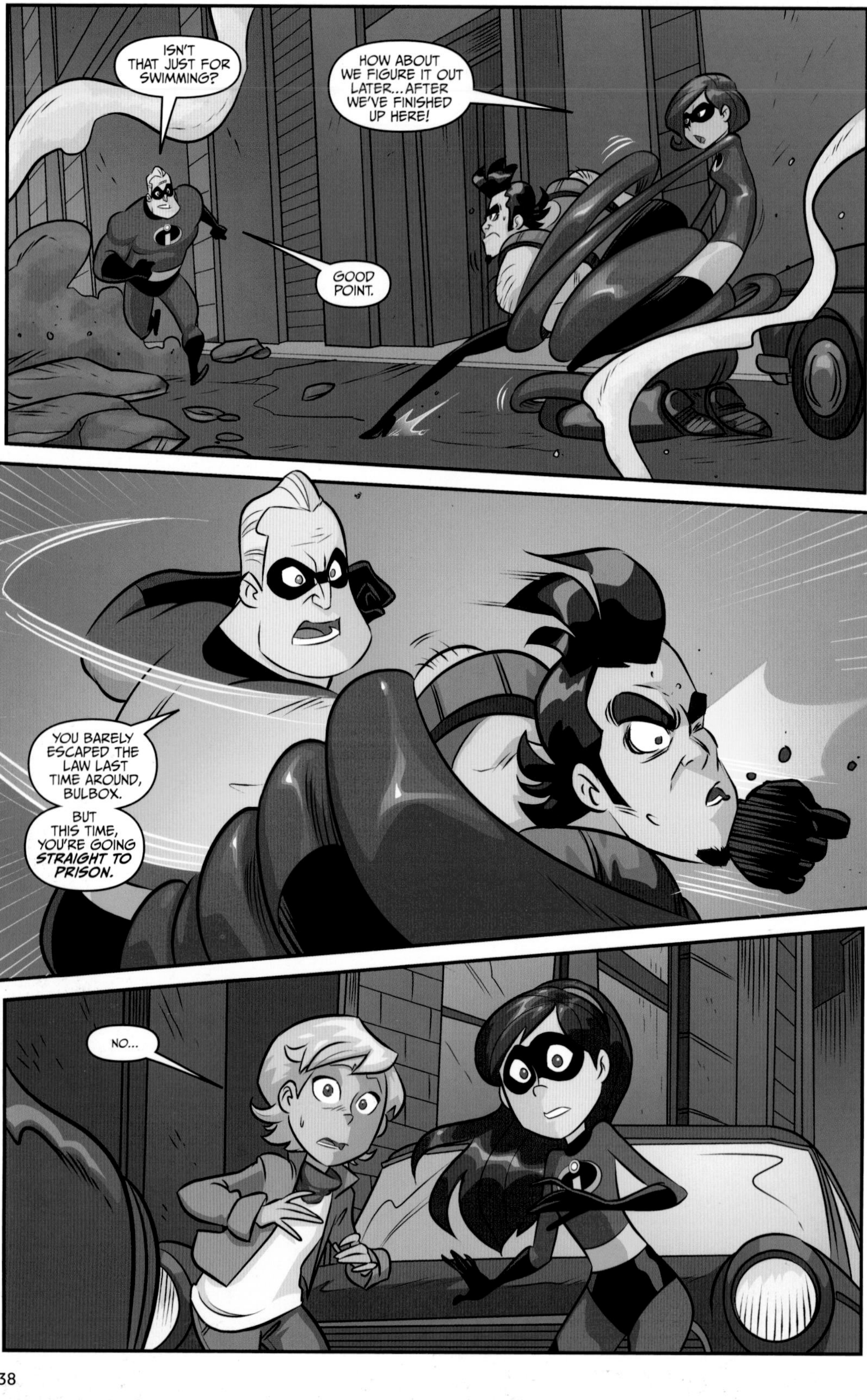
ISN'T THAT JUST FOR SWIMMING?
HOW ABOUT WE FIGURE IT OUT LATER...AFTER WE'VE FINISHED UP HERE!
GOOD POINT.
YOU BARELY ESCAPED THE LAW LAST TIME AROUND, BULBOX.
BUT THIS TIME, YOU'RE GOING **STRAIGHT TO PRISON.**
NO...

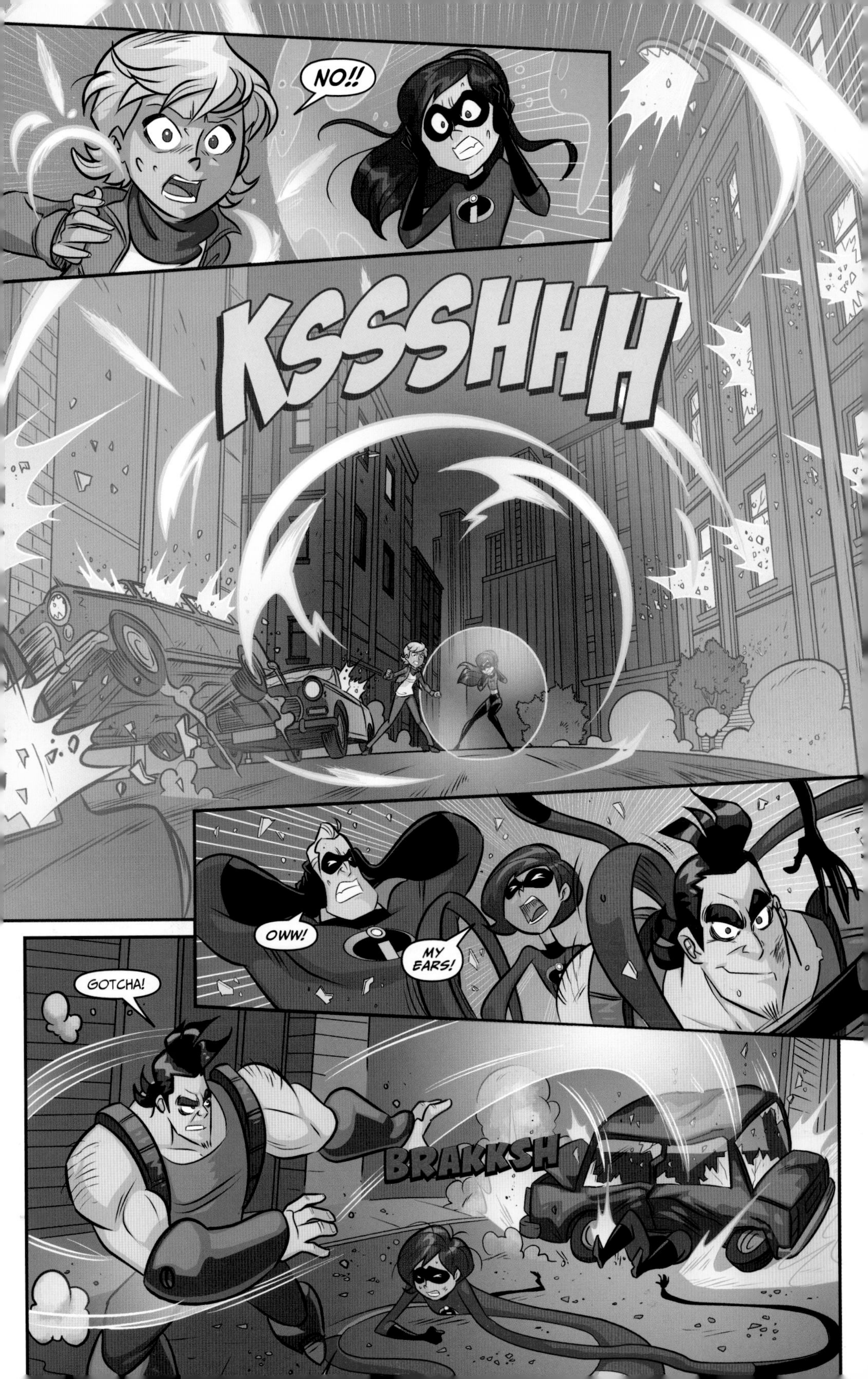
NO!!
KSSSHHH
OWW!
MY EARS!
GOTCHA!

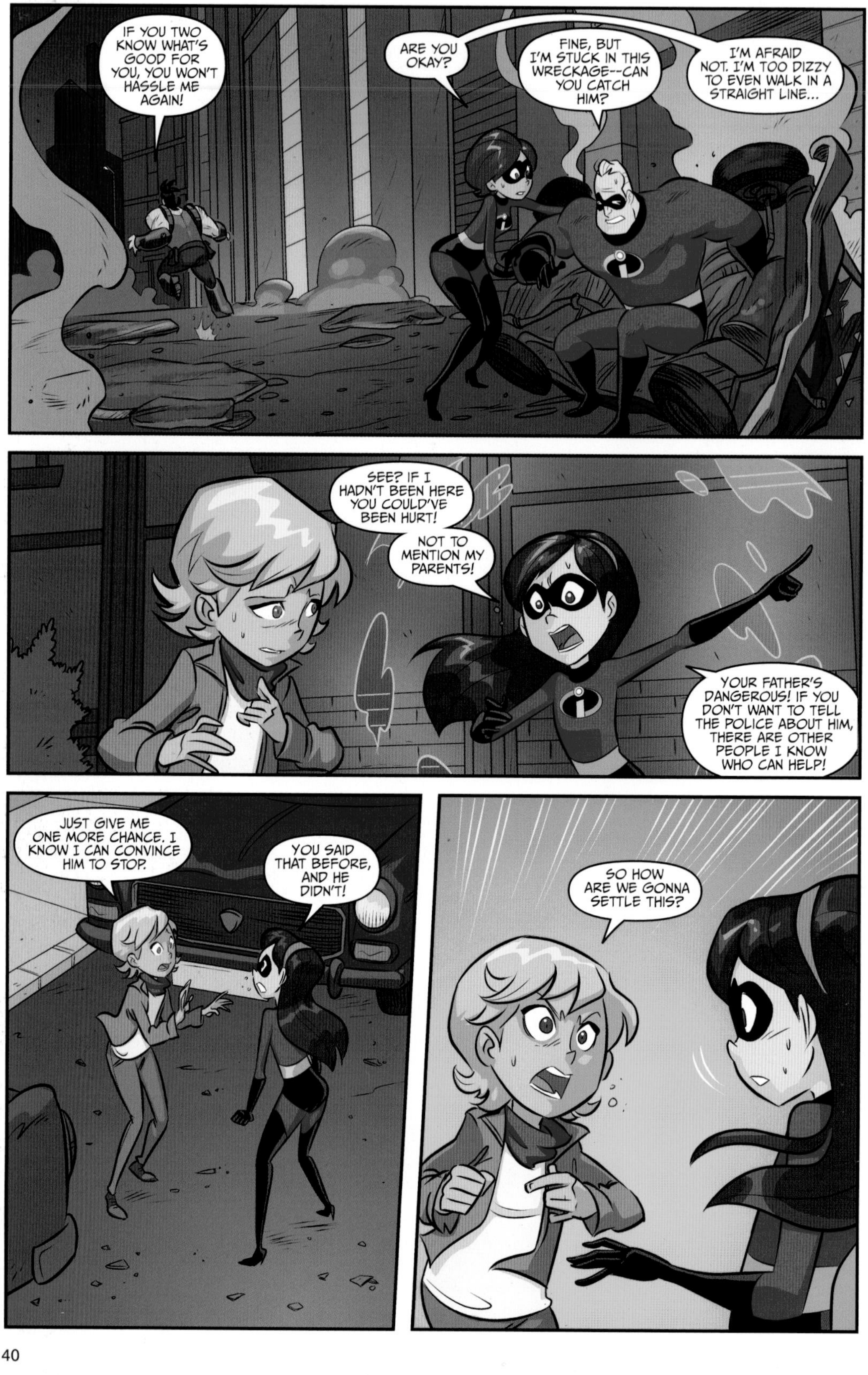
IF YOU TWO KNOW WHAT'S GOOD FOR YOU, YOU WON'T HASSLE ME AGAIN!
ARE YOU OKAY?
FINE, BUT I'M STUCK IN THIS WRECKAGE--CAN YOU CATCH HIM?
I'M AFRAID NOT. I'M TOO DIZZY TO EVEN WALK IN A STRAIGHT LINE...
SEE? IF I HADN'T BEEN HERE YOU COULD'VE BEEN HURT!
NOT TO MENTION MY PARENTS!
YOUR FATHER'S DANGEROUS! IF YOU DON'T WANT TO TELL THE POLICE ABOUT HIM, THERE ARE OTHER PEOPLE I KNOW WHO CAN HELP!
JUST GIVE ME ONE MORE CHANCE. I KNOW I CAN CONVINCE HIM TO STOP.
YOU SAID THAT BEFORE, AND HE DIDN'T!
SO HOW ARE WE GONNA SETTLE THIS?

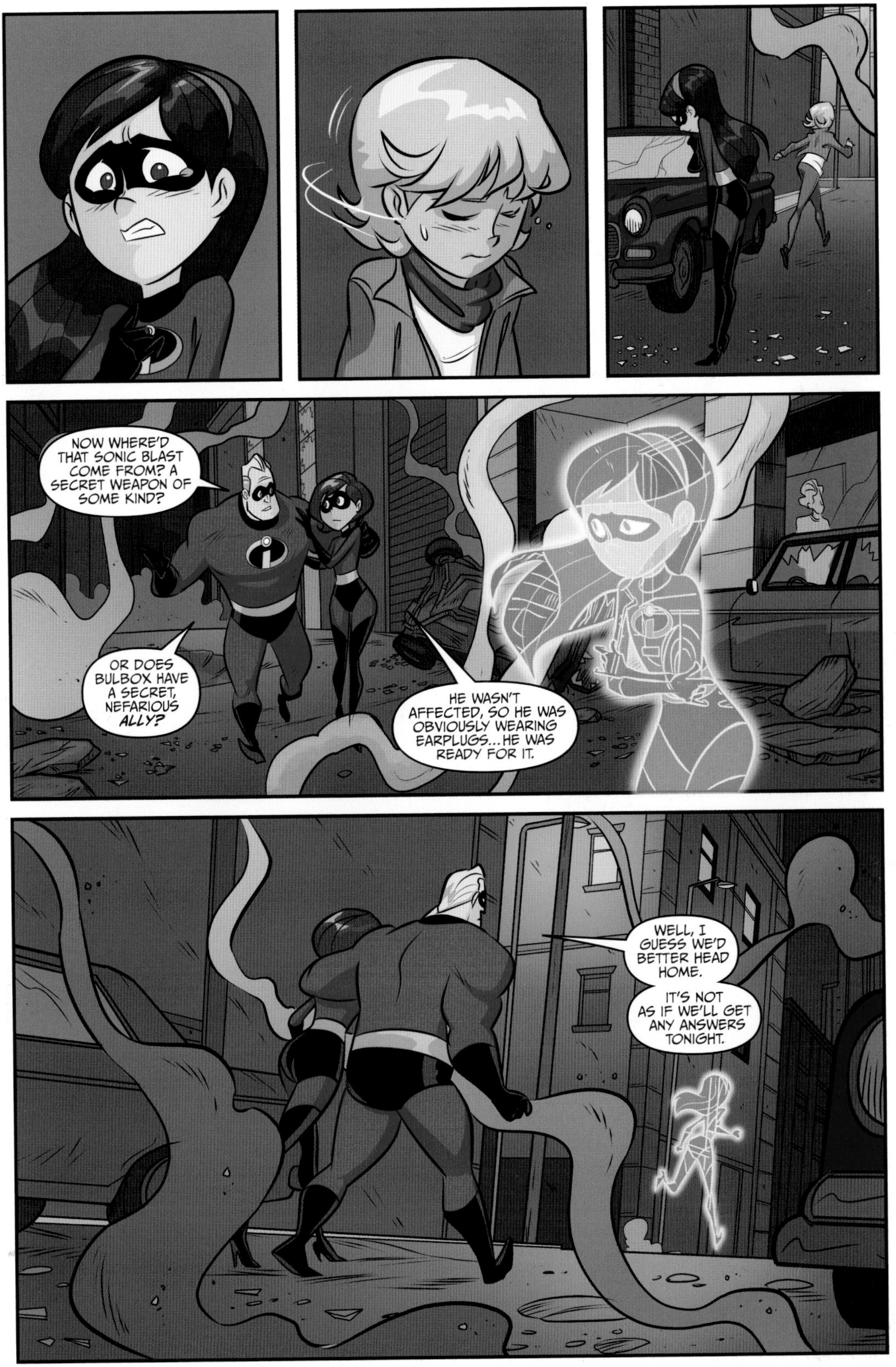
NOW WHERE'D THAT SONIC BLAST COME FROM? A SECRET WEAPON OF SOME KIND?
OR DOES BULBOX HAVE A SECRET, NEFARIOUS *ALLY?*
HE WASN'T AFFECTED, SO HE WAS OBVIOUSLY WEARING EARPLUGS...HE WAS READY FOR IT.
WELL, I GUESS WE'D BETTER HEAD HOME.
IT'S NOT AS IF WE'LL GET ANY ANSWERS TONIGHT.

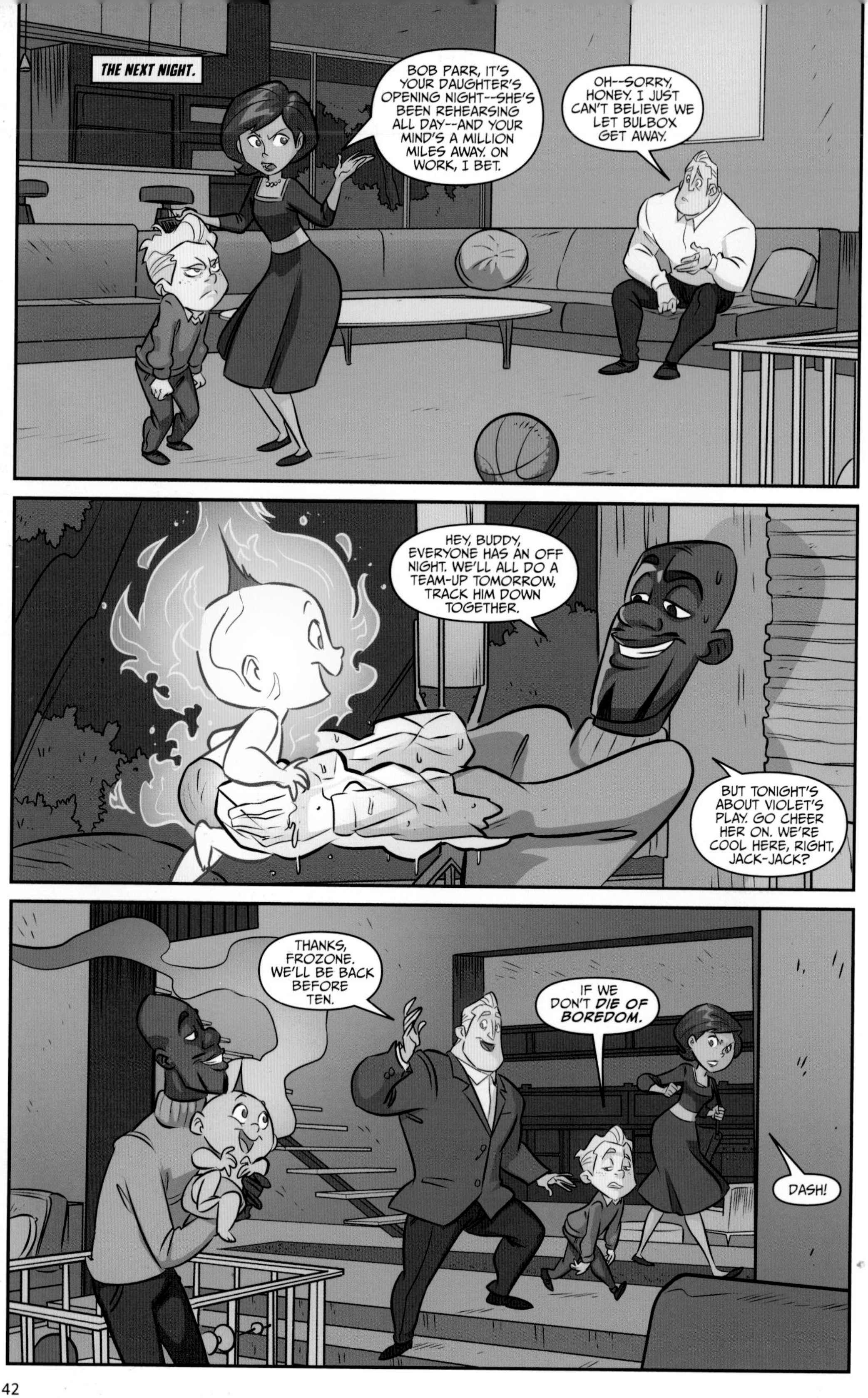
THE NEXT NIGHT.
BOB PARR, IT'S YOUR DAUGHTER'S OPENING NIGHT--SHE'S BEEN REHEARSING ALL DAY--AND YOUR MIND'S A MILLION MILES AWAY. ON WORK, I BET.
OH--SORRY, HONEY. I JUST CAN'T BELIEVE WE LET BULBOX GET AWAY.
HEY, BUDDY, EVERYONE HAS AN OFF NIGHT. WE'LL ALL DO A TEAM-UP TOMORROW, TRACK HIM DOWN TOGETHER.
BUT TONIGHT'S ABOUT VIOLET'S PLAY. GO CHEER HER ON. WE'RE COOL HERE, RIGHT, JACK-JACK?
THANKS, FROZONE. WE'LL BE BACK BEFORE TEN.
IF WE DON'T *DIE OF BOREDOM.*
DASH!

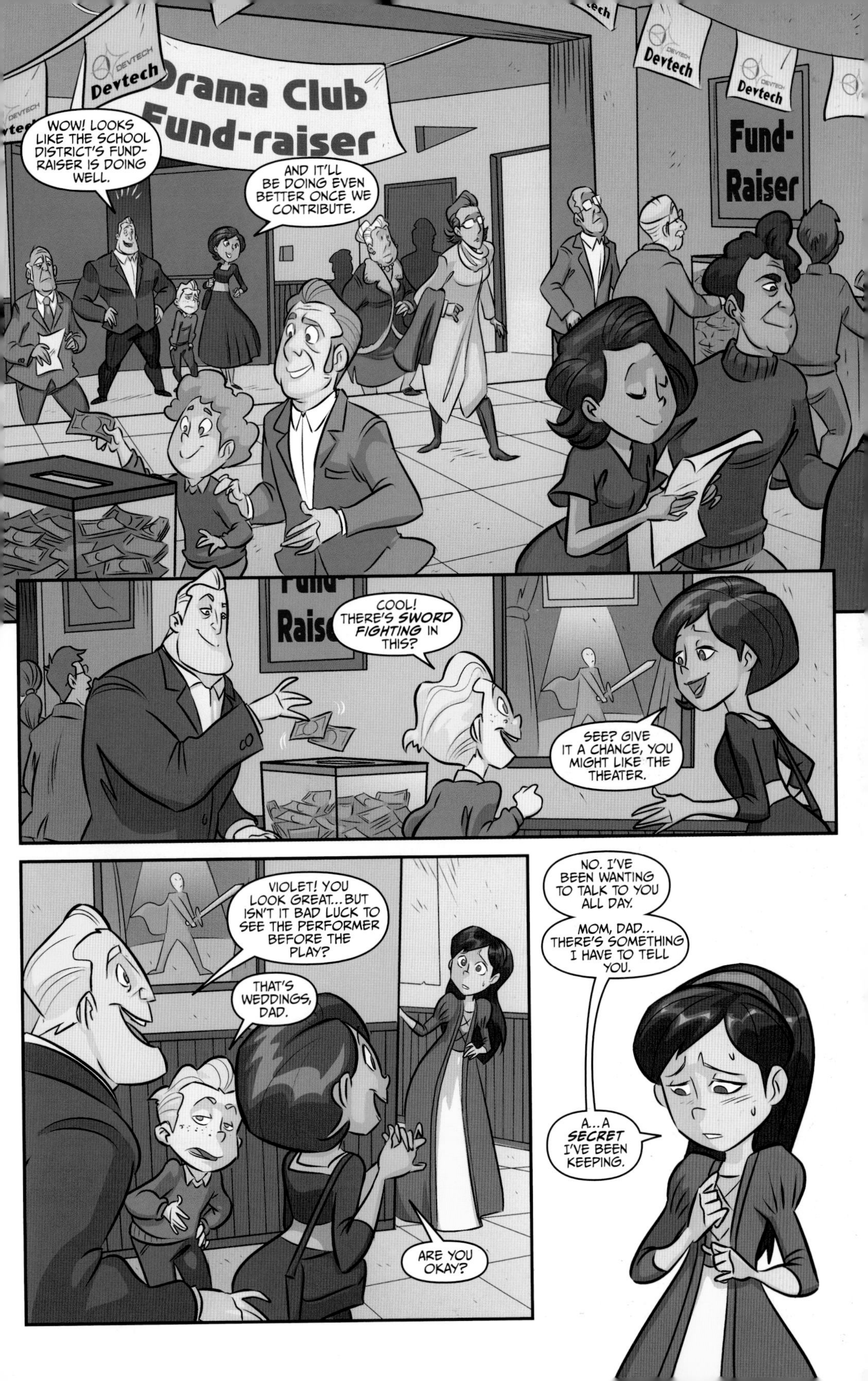
Devtech
Drama Club Fund-raiser
Devtech
Fund-Raiser
WOW! LOOKS LIKE THE SCHOOL DISTRICT'S FUND-RAISER IS DOING WELL.
AND IT'LL BE DOING EVEN BETTER ONCE WE CONTRIBUTE.
COOL! THERE'S SWORD FIGHTING IN THIS?
SEE? GIVE IT A CHANCE, YOU MIGHT LIKE THE THEATER.
VIOLET! YOU LOOK GREAT... BUT ISN'T IT BAD LUCK TO SEE THE PERFORMER BEFORE THE PLAY?
THAT'S WEDDINGS, DAD.
ARE YOU OKAY?
NO. I'VE BEEN WANTING TO TALK TO YOU ALL DAY.
MOM, DAD... THERE'S SOMETHING I HAVE TO TELL YOU.
A... A SECRET I'VE BEEN KEEPING.

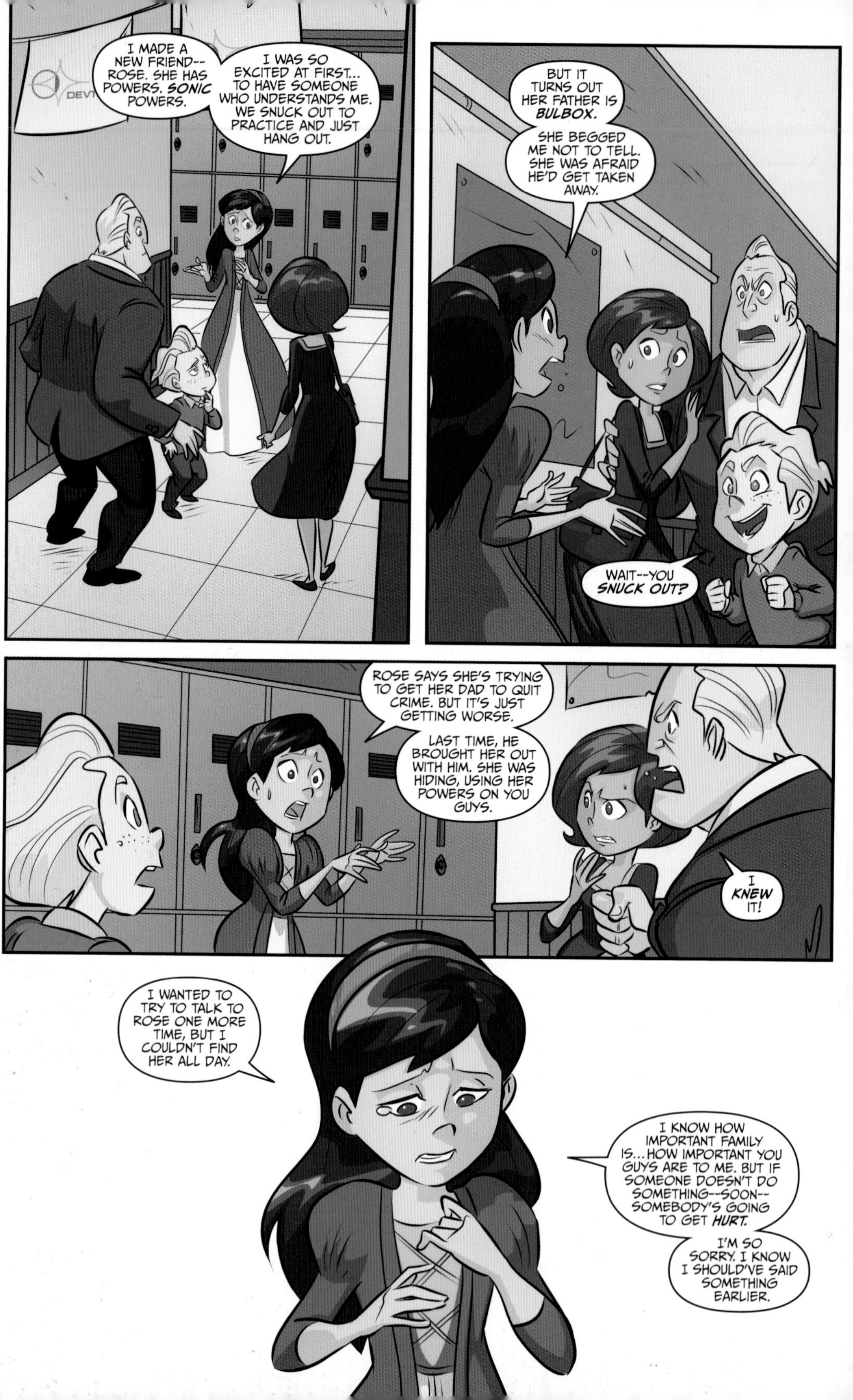
DEVT
I MADE A NEW FRIEND-- ROSE. SHE HAS POWERS. SONIC POWERS.
I WAS SO EXCITED AT FIRST... TO HAVE SOMEONE WHO UNDERSTANDS ME. WE SNUCK OUT TO PRACTICE AND JUST HANG OUT.
BUT IT TURNS OUT HER FATHER IS BULBOX.
SHE BEGGED ME NOT TO TELL. SHE WAS AFRAID HE'D GET TAKEN AWAY.
WAIT--YOU SNUCK OUT?
ROSE SAYS SHE'S TRYING TO GET HER DAD TO QUIT CRIME. BUT IT'S JUST GETTING WORSE.
LAST TIME, HE BROUGHT HER OUT WITH HIM. SHE WAS HIDING, USING HER POWERS ON YOU GUYS.
I KNEW IT!
I WANTED TO TRY TO TALK TO ROSE ONE MORE TIME, BUT I COULDN'T FIND HER ALL DAY.
I KNOW HOW IMPORTANT FAMILY IS...HOW IMPORTANT YOU GUYS ARE TO ME. BUT IF SOMEONE DOESN'T DO SOMETHING--SOON-- SOMEBODY'S GOING TO GET HURT.
I'M SO SORRY. I KNOW I SHOULD'VE SAID SOMETHING EARLIER.

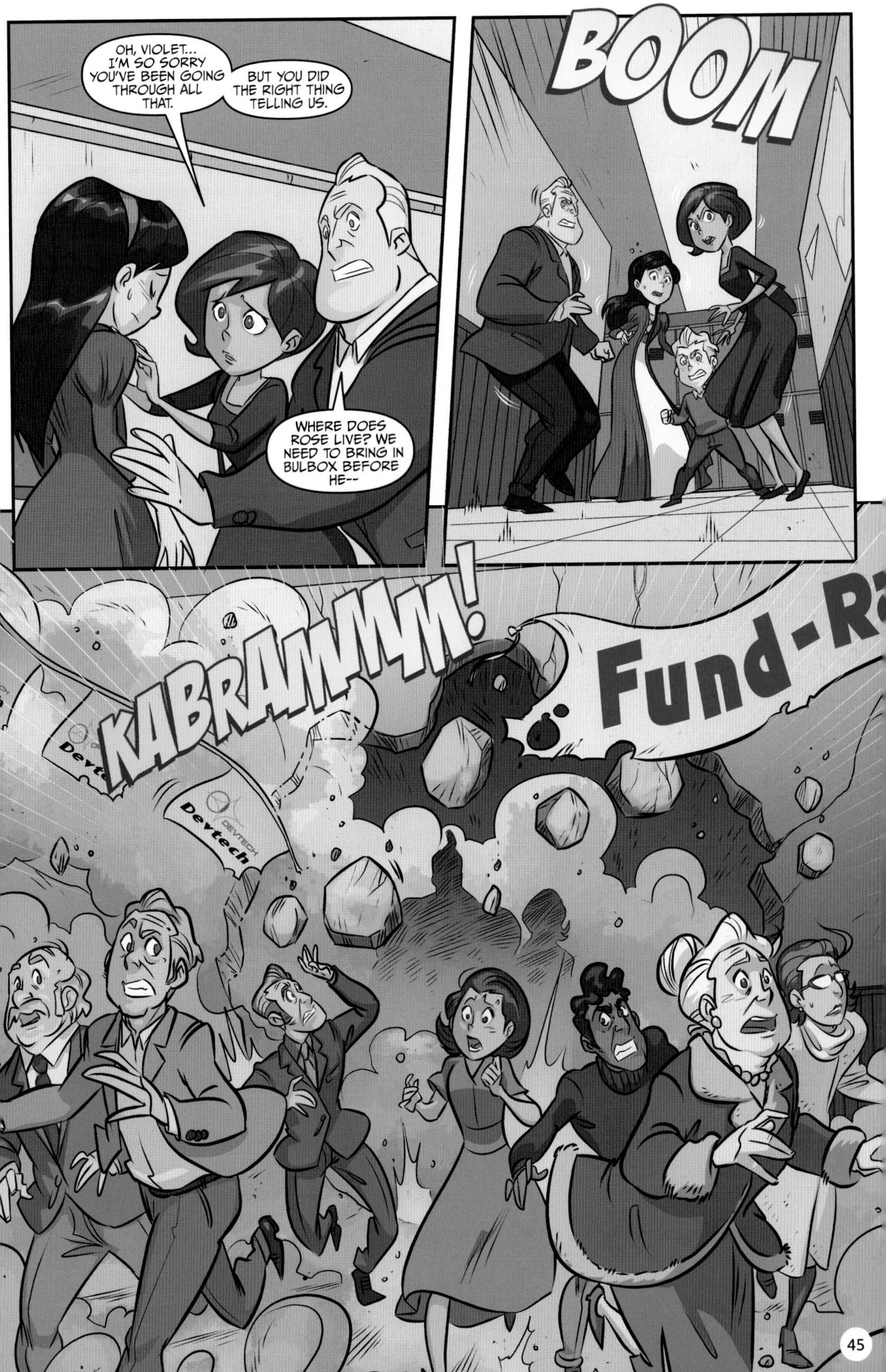

OH, VIOLET... I'M SO SORRY YOU'VE BEEN GOING THROUGH ALL THAT.
BUT YOU DID THE RIGHT THING TELLING US.
WHERE DOES ROSE LIVE? WE NEED TO BRING IN BULBOX BEFORE HE--
BOOM
KABRAMMM!
Fund-Ra
Devtech
DEVTECH
Devtech

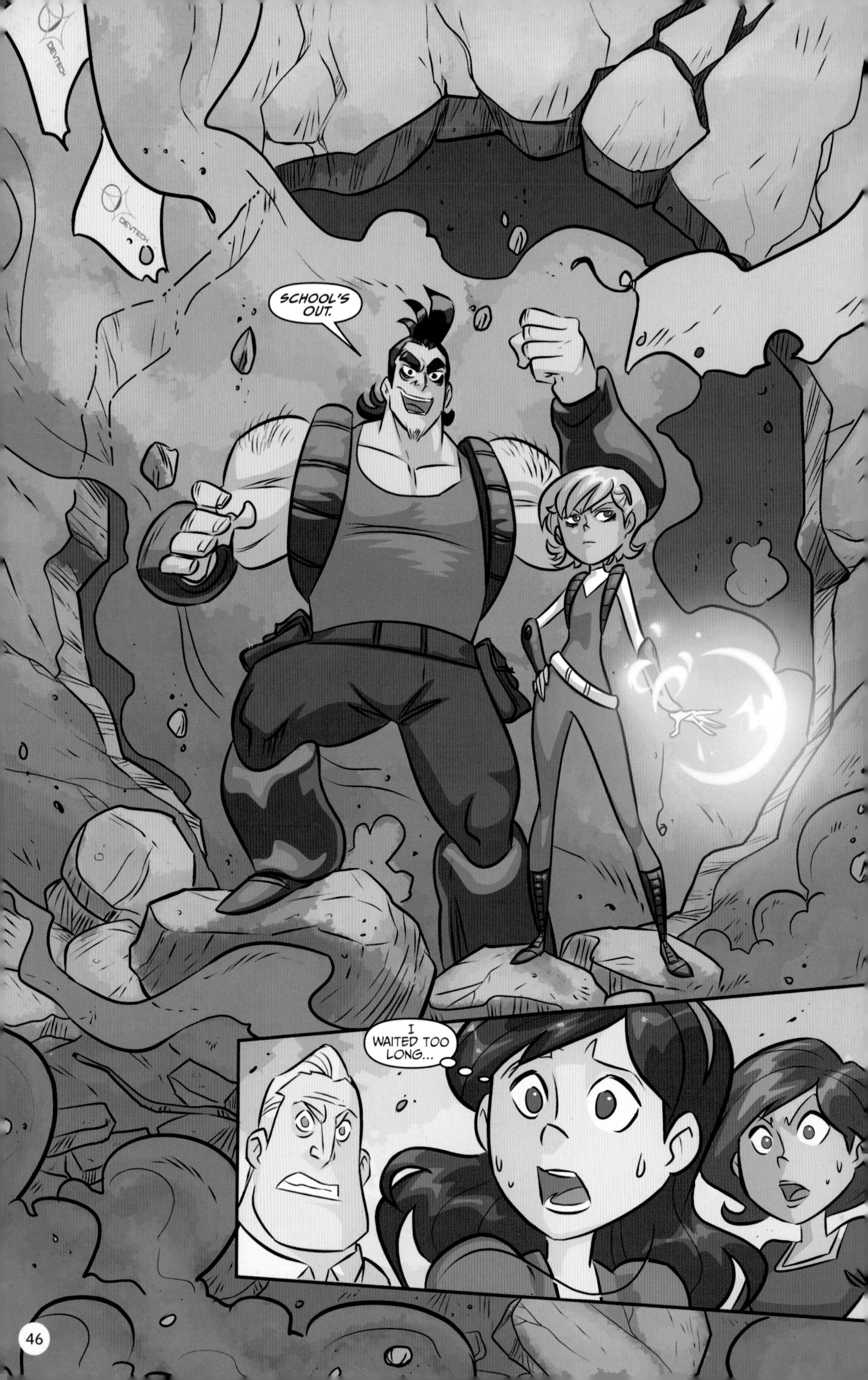
DEVTECH
DEVTECH
SCHOOL'S OUT.
I WAITED TOO LONG...

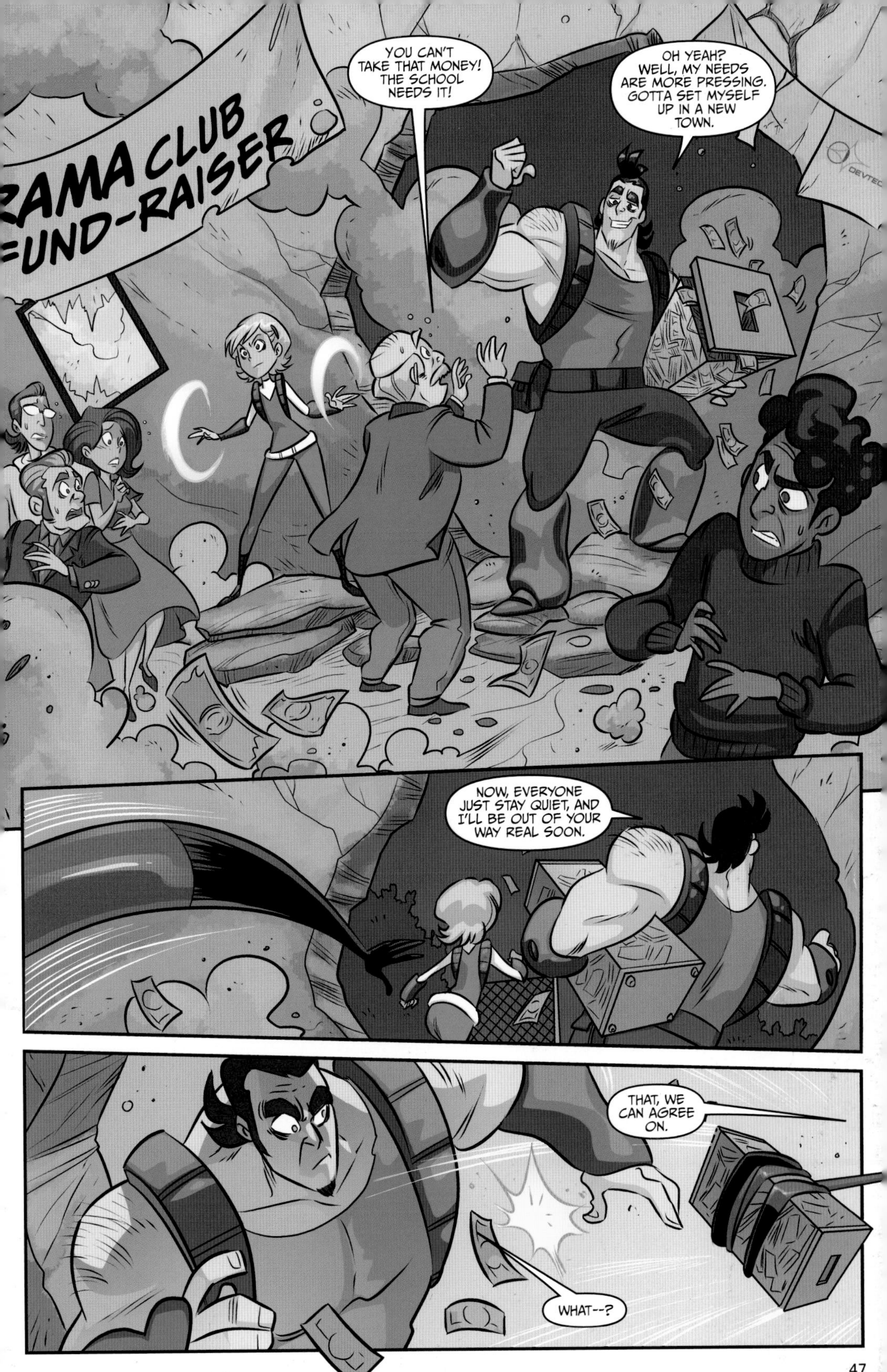

RAMA CLUB
FUND-RAISER
YOU CAN'T TAKE THAT MONEY! THE SCHOOL NEEDS IT!
OH YEAH? WELL, MY NEEDS ARE MORE PRESSING. GOTTA SET MYSELF UP IN A NEW TOWN.
NOW, EVERYONE JUST STAY QUIET, AND I'LL BE OUT OF YOUR WAY REAL SOON.
THAT, WE CAN AGREE ON.
WHAT--?

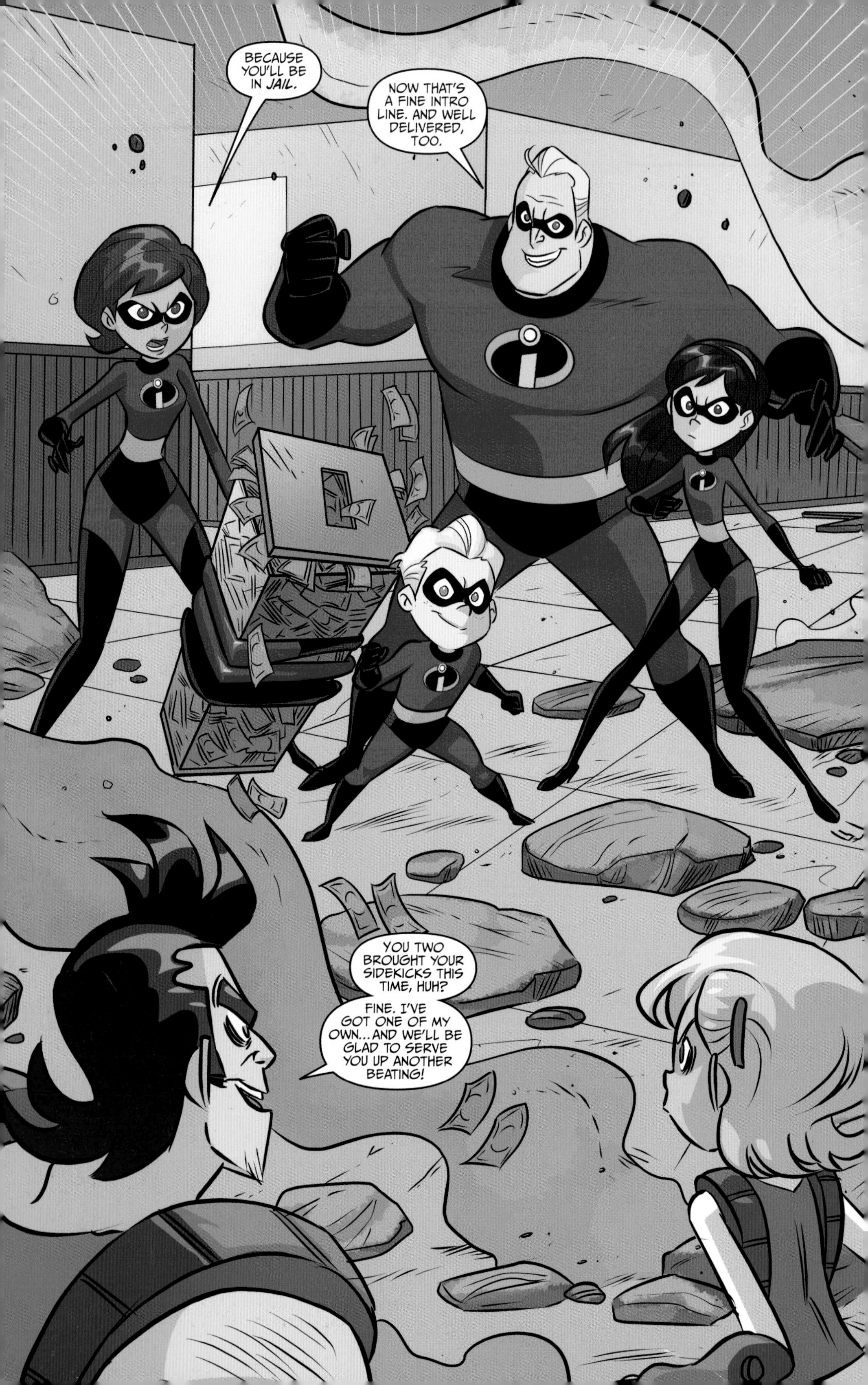
BECAUSE YOU'LL BE IN *JAIL.*
NOW THAT'S A FINE INTRO LINE. AND WELL DELIVERED, TOO.
YOU TWO BROUGHT YOUR SIDEKICKS THIS TIME, HUH?
FINE. I'VE GOT ONE OF MY OWN...AND WE'LL BE GLAD TO SERVE YOU UP ANOTHER BEATING!

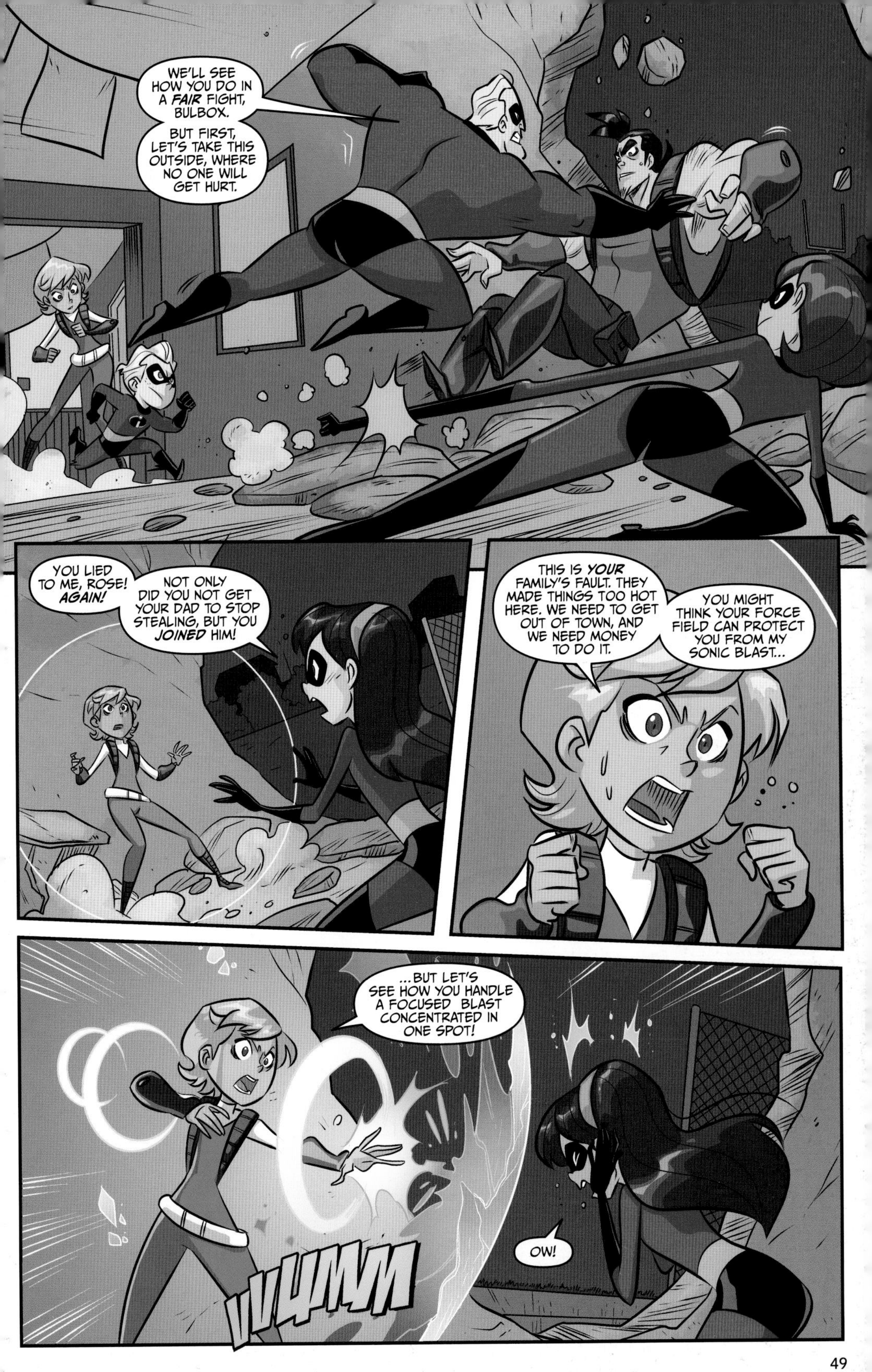

WE'LL SEE HOW YOU DO IN A *FAIR* FIGHT, BULBOX.
BUT FIRST, LET'S TAKE THIS OUTSIDE, WHERE NO ONE WILL GET HURT.
YOU LIED TO ME, ROSE! *AGAIN!*
NOT ONLY DID YOU NOT GET YOUR DAD TO STOP STEALING, BUT YOU *JOINED* HIM!
THIS IS *YOUR* FAMILY'S FAULT. THEY MADE THINGS TOO HOT HERE. WE NEED TO GET OUT OF TOWN, AND WE NEED MONEY TO DO IT.
YOU MIGHT THINK YOUR FORCE FIELD CAN PROTECT YOU FROM MY SONIC BLAST...
...BUT LET'S SEE HOW YOU HANDLE A FOCUSED BLAST CONCENTRATED IN ONE SPOT!
VVUMMM
OW!

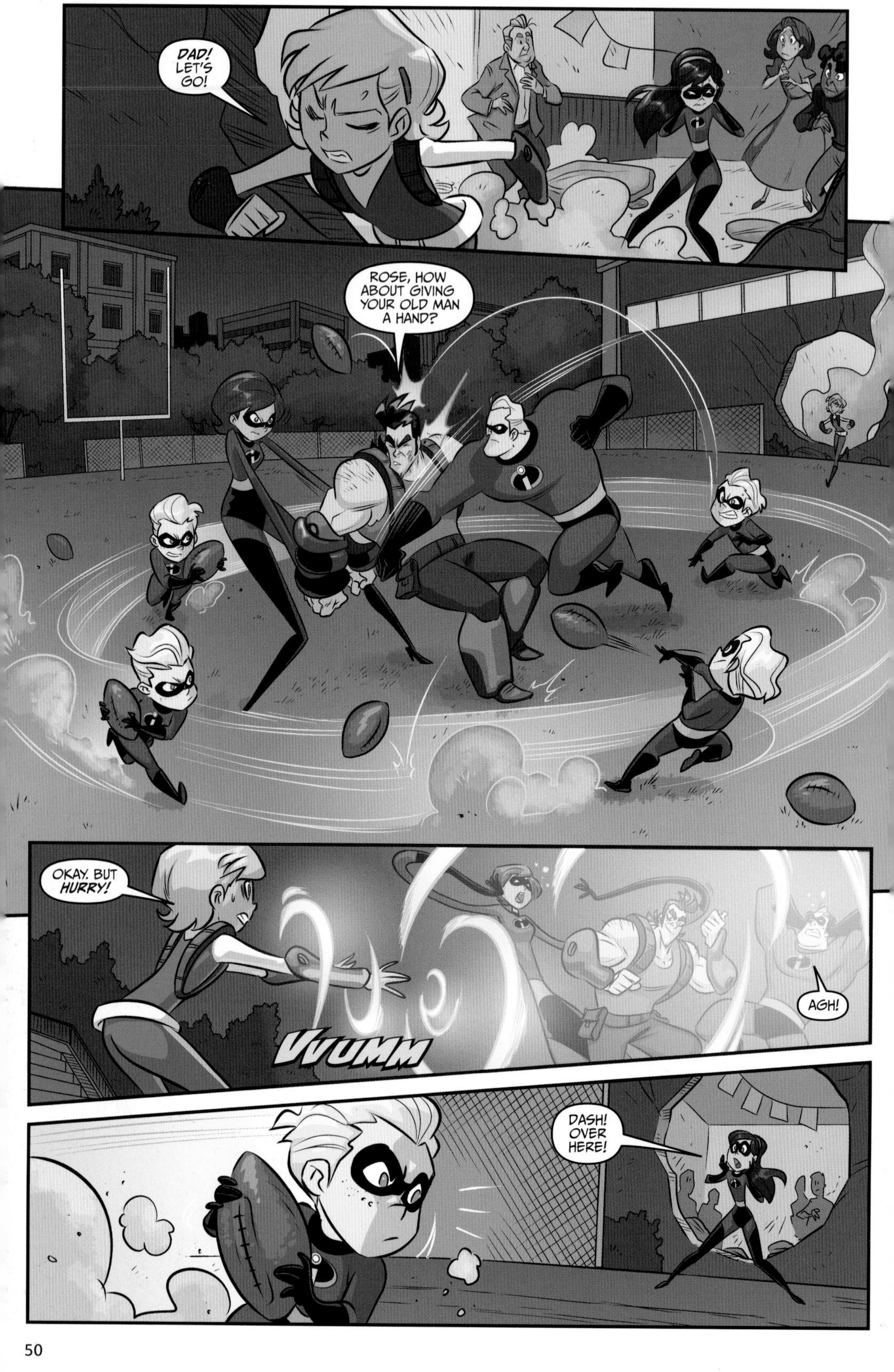
DAD! LET'S GO!
ROSE, HOW ABOUT GIVING YOUR OLD MAN A HAND?
OKAY. BUT *HURRY!*
VVUMM
AGH!
DASH! OVER HERE!

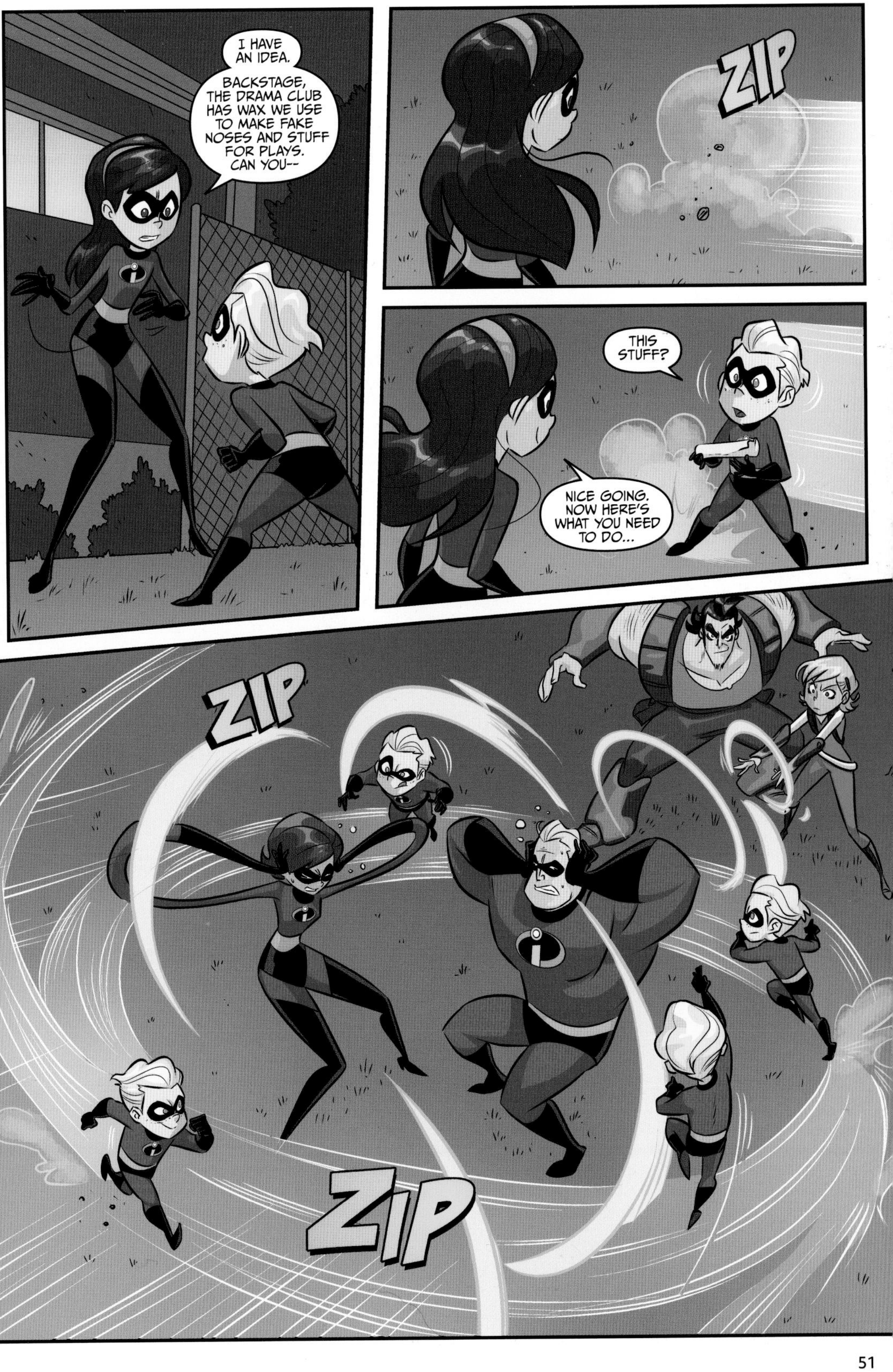
I HAVE AN IDEA.
BACKSTAGE, THE DRAMA CLUB HAS WAX WE USE TO MAKE FAKE NOSES AND STUFF FOR PLAYS. CAN YOU--
ZIP
THIS STUFF?
NICE GOING. NOW HERE'S WHAT YOU NEED TO DO...
ZIP
ZIP

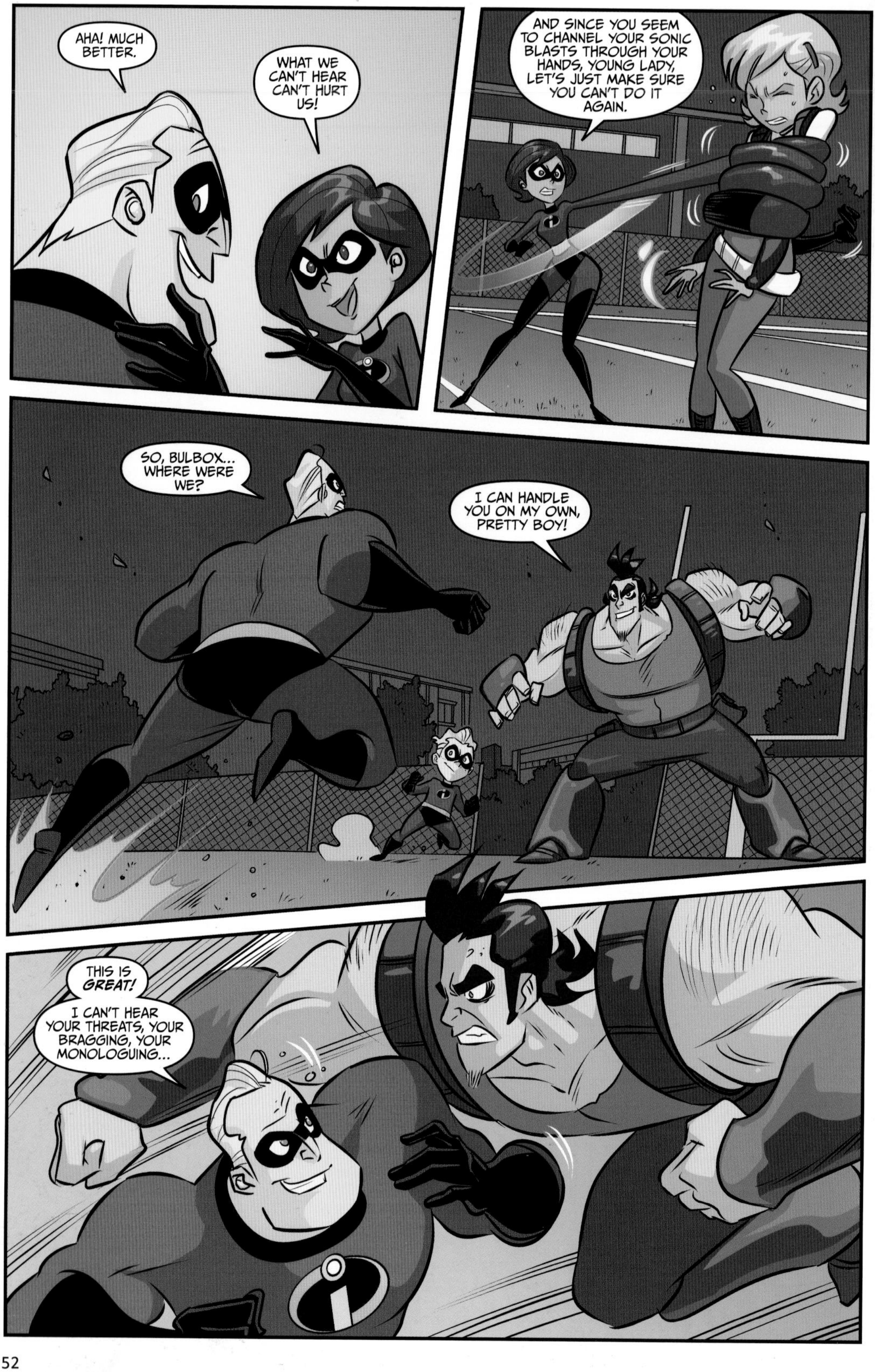
AHA! MUCH BETTER.
WHAT WE CAN'T HEAR CAN'T HURT US!
AND SINCE YOU SEEM TO CHANNEL YOUR SONIC BLASTS THROUGH YOUR HANDS, YOUNG LADY, LET'S JUST MAKE SURE YOU CAN'T DO IT AGAIN.
SO, BULBOX... WHERE WERE WE?
I CAN HANDLE YOU ON MY OWN, PRETTY BOY!
THIS IS GREAT!
I CAN'T HEAR YOUR THREATS, YOUR BRAGGING, YOUR MONOLOGUING...

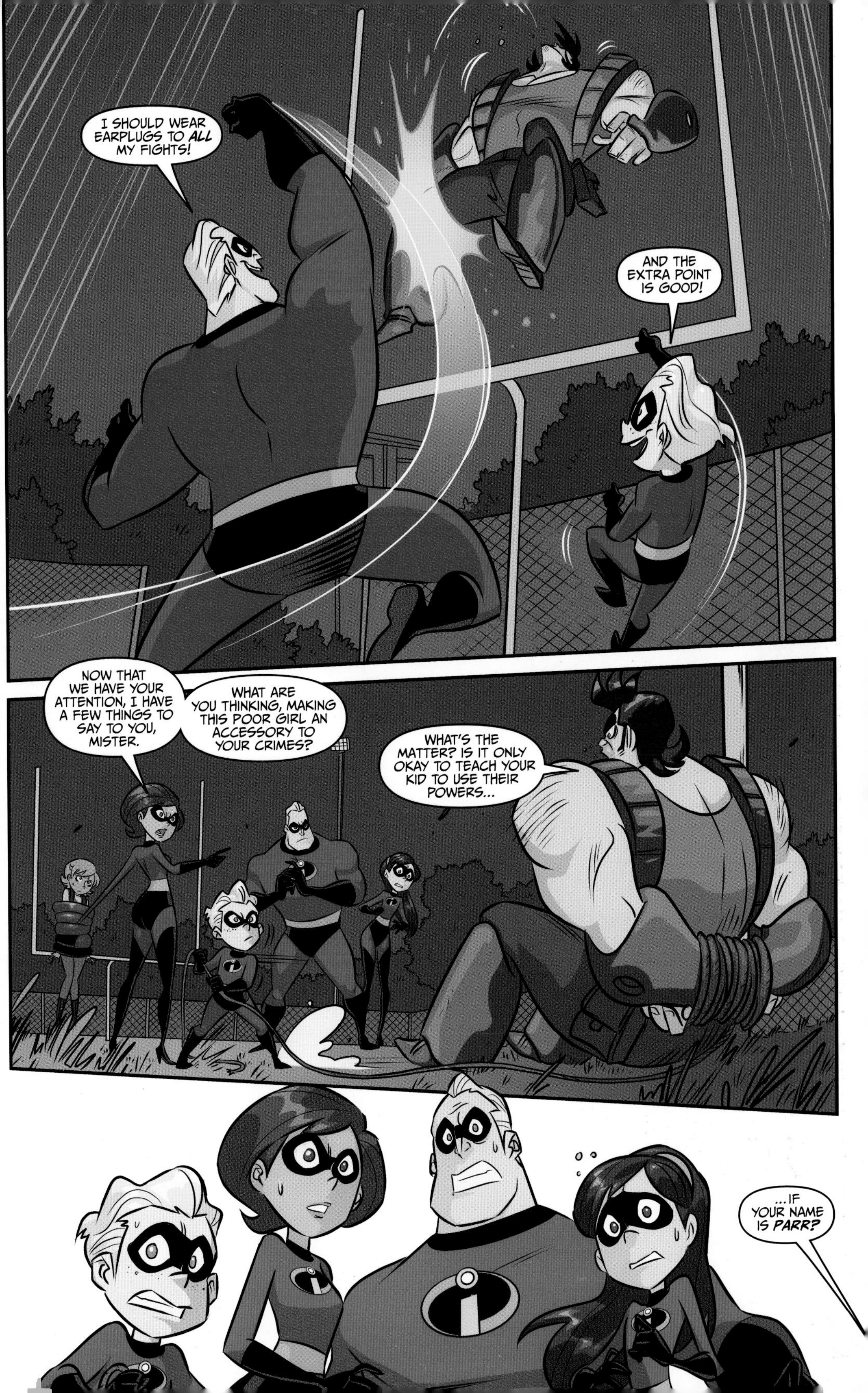
I SHOULD WEAR EARPLUGS TO ALL MY FIGHTS!
AND THE EXTRA POINT IS GOOD!
NOW THAT WE HAVE YOUR ATTENTION, I HAVE A FEW THINGS TO SAY TO YOU, MISTER.
WHAT ARE YOU THINKING, MAKING THIS POOR GIRL AN ACCESSORY TO YOUR CRIMES?
WHAT'S THE MATTER? IS IT ONLY OKAY TO TEACH YOUR KID TO USE THEIR POWERS...
...IF YOUR NAME IS PARR?

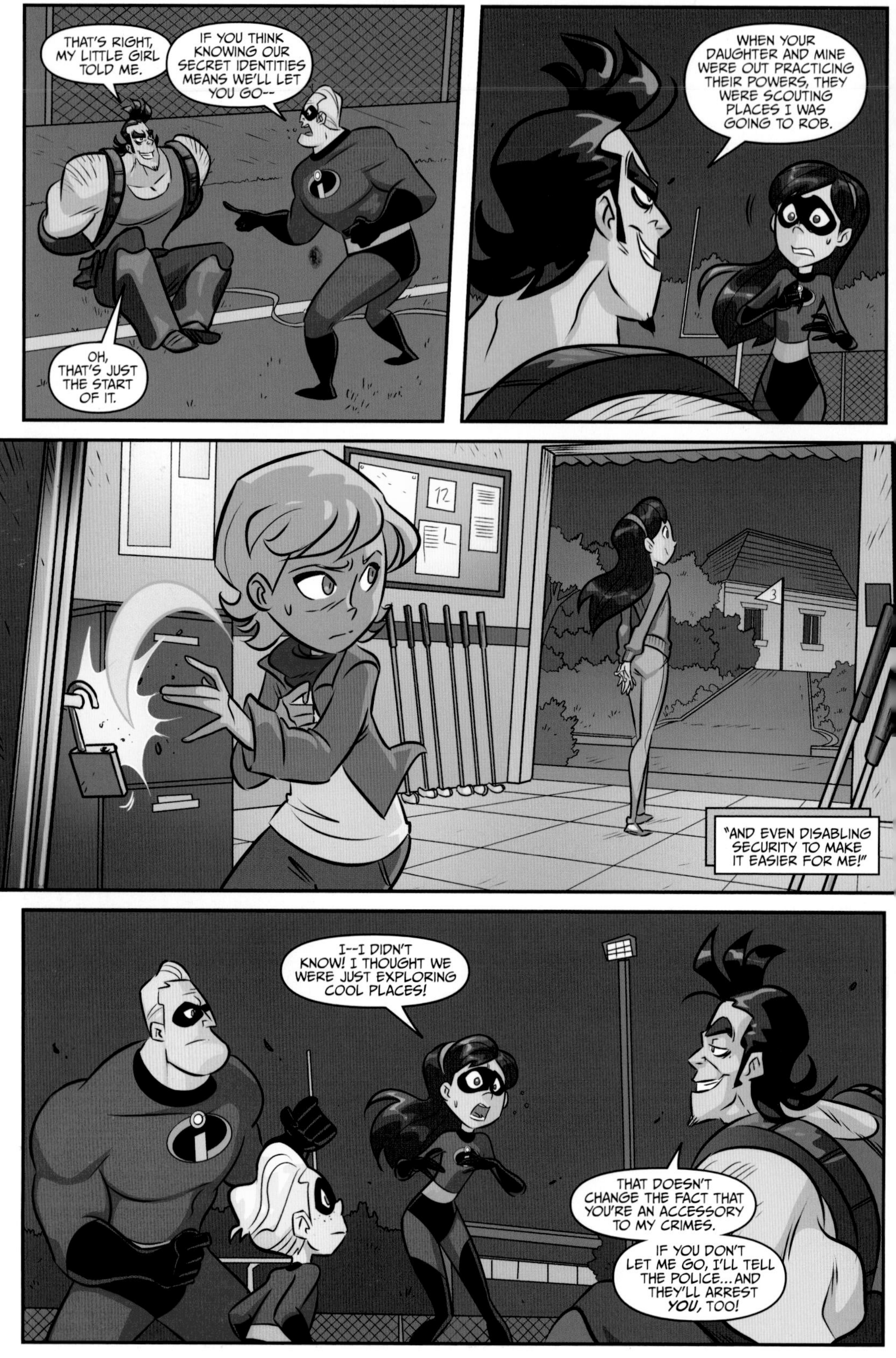
THAT'S RIGHT, MY LITTLE GIRL TOLD ME.
IF YOU THINK KNOWING OUR SECRET IDENTITIES MEANS WE'LL LET YOU GO--
OH, THAT'S JUST THE START OF IT.
WHEN YOUR DAUGHTER AND MINE WERE OUT PRACTICING THEIR POWERS, THEY WERE SCOUTING PLACES I WAS GOING TO ROB.
12
3
"AND EVEN DISABLING SECURITY TO MAKE IT EASIER FOR ME!"
I--I DIDN'T KNOW! I THOUGHT WE WERE JUST EXPLORING COOL PLACES!
THAT DOESN'T CHANGE THE FACT THAT YOU'RE AN ACCESSORY TO MY CRIMES.
IF YOU DON'T LET ME GO, I'LL TELL THE POLICE...AND THEY'LL ARREST *YOU*, TOO!

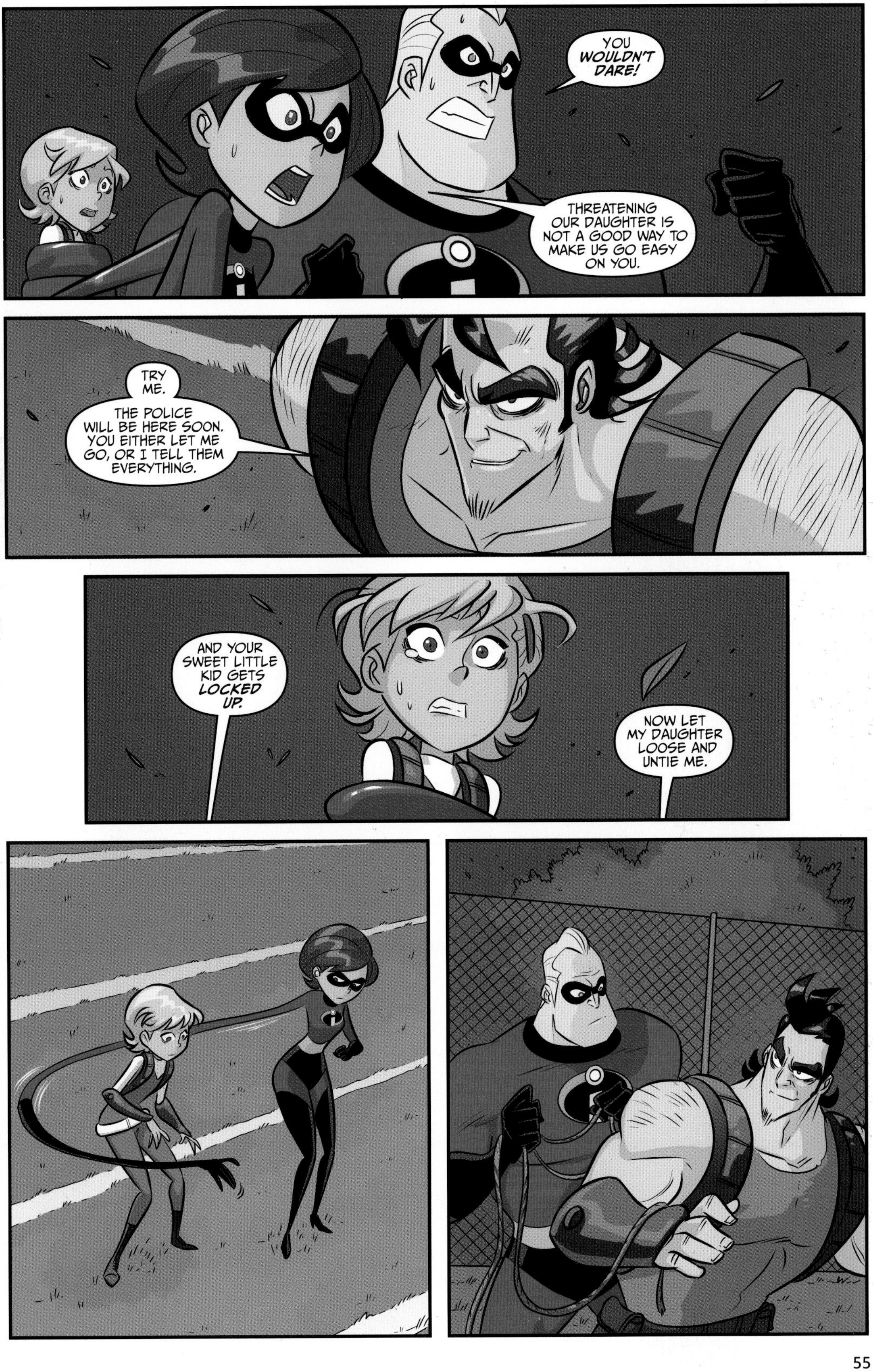
YOU *WOULDN'T DARE!*
THREATENING OUR DAUGHTER IS NOT A GOOD WAY TO MAKE US GO EASY ON YOU.
TRY ME.
THE POLICE WILL BE HERE SOON. YOU EITHER LET ME GO, OR I TELL THEM EVERYTHING.
AND YOUR SWEET LITTLE KID GETS *LOCKED UP.*
NOW LET MY DAUGHTER LOOSE AND UNTIE ME.

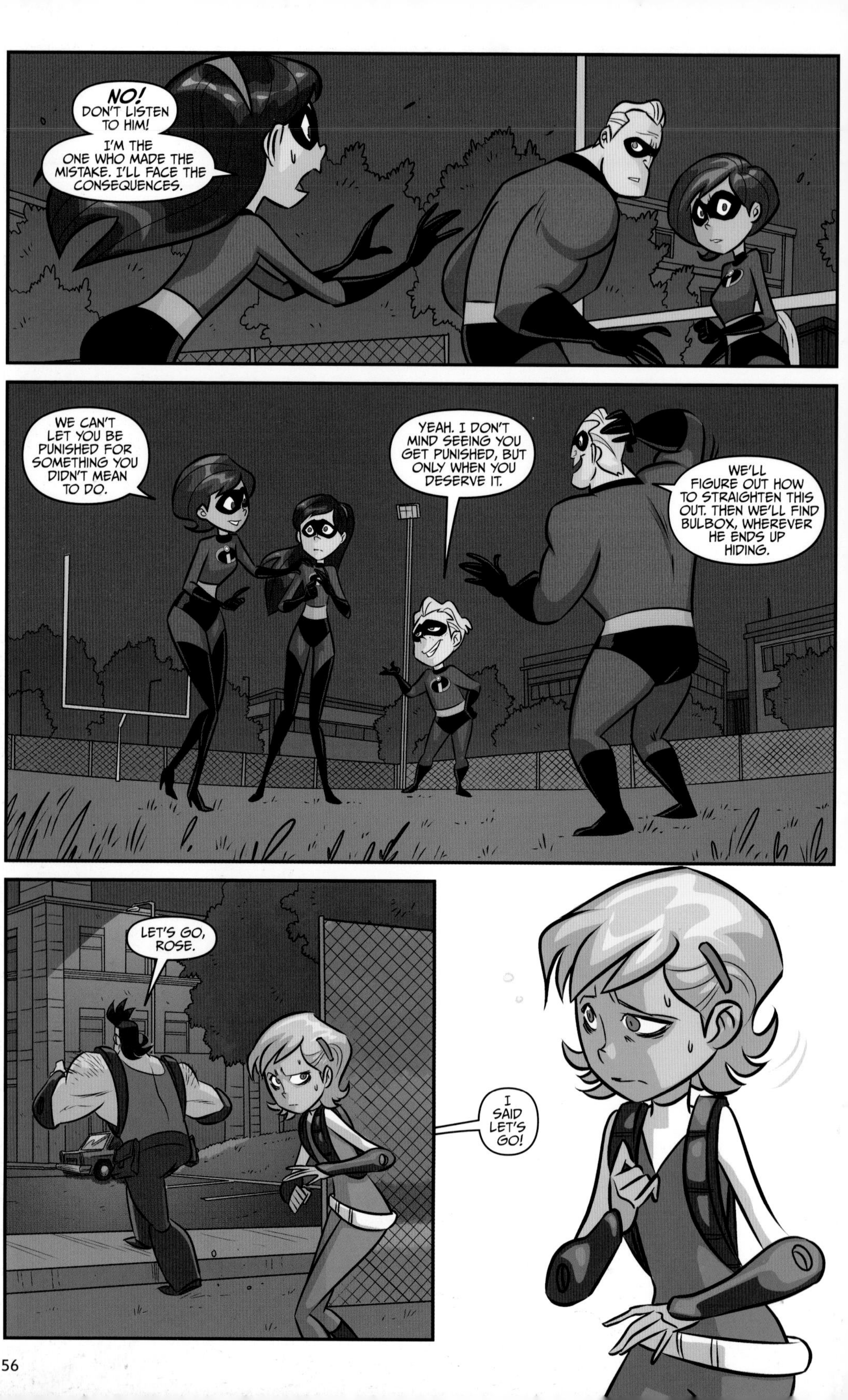
NO! DON'T LISTEN TO HIM!
I'M THE ONE WHO MADE THE MISTAKE. I'LL FACE THE CONSEQUENCES.
WE CAN'T LET YOU BE PUNISHED FOR SOMETHING YOU DIDN'T MEAN TO DO.
YEAH. I DON'T MIND SEEING YOU GET PUNISHED, BUT ONLY WHEN YOU DESERVE IT.
WE'LL FIGURE OUT HOW TO STRAIGHTEN THIS OUT. THEN WE'LL FIND BULBOX, WHEREVER HE ENDS UP HIDING.
LET'S GO, ROSE.
I SAID LET'S GO!

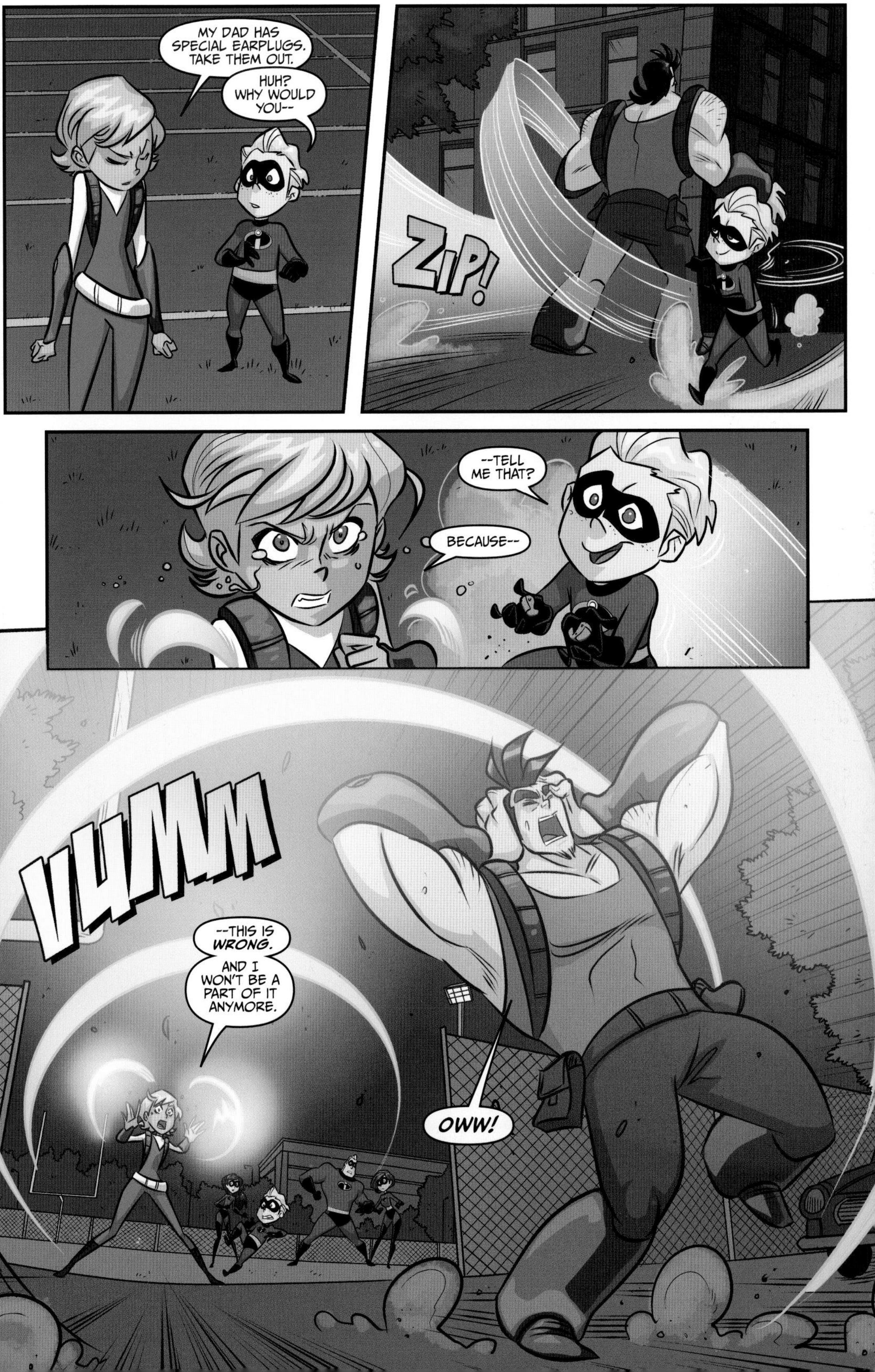
MY DAD HAS SPECIAL EARPLUGS. TAKE THEM OUT.
HUH? WHY WOULD YOU--
ZIP!
--TELL ME THAT?
BECAUSE--
VUMM
--THIS IS WRONG.
AND I WON'T BE A PART OF IT ANYMORE.
OWW!

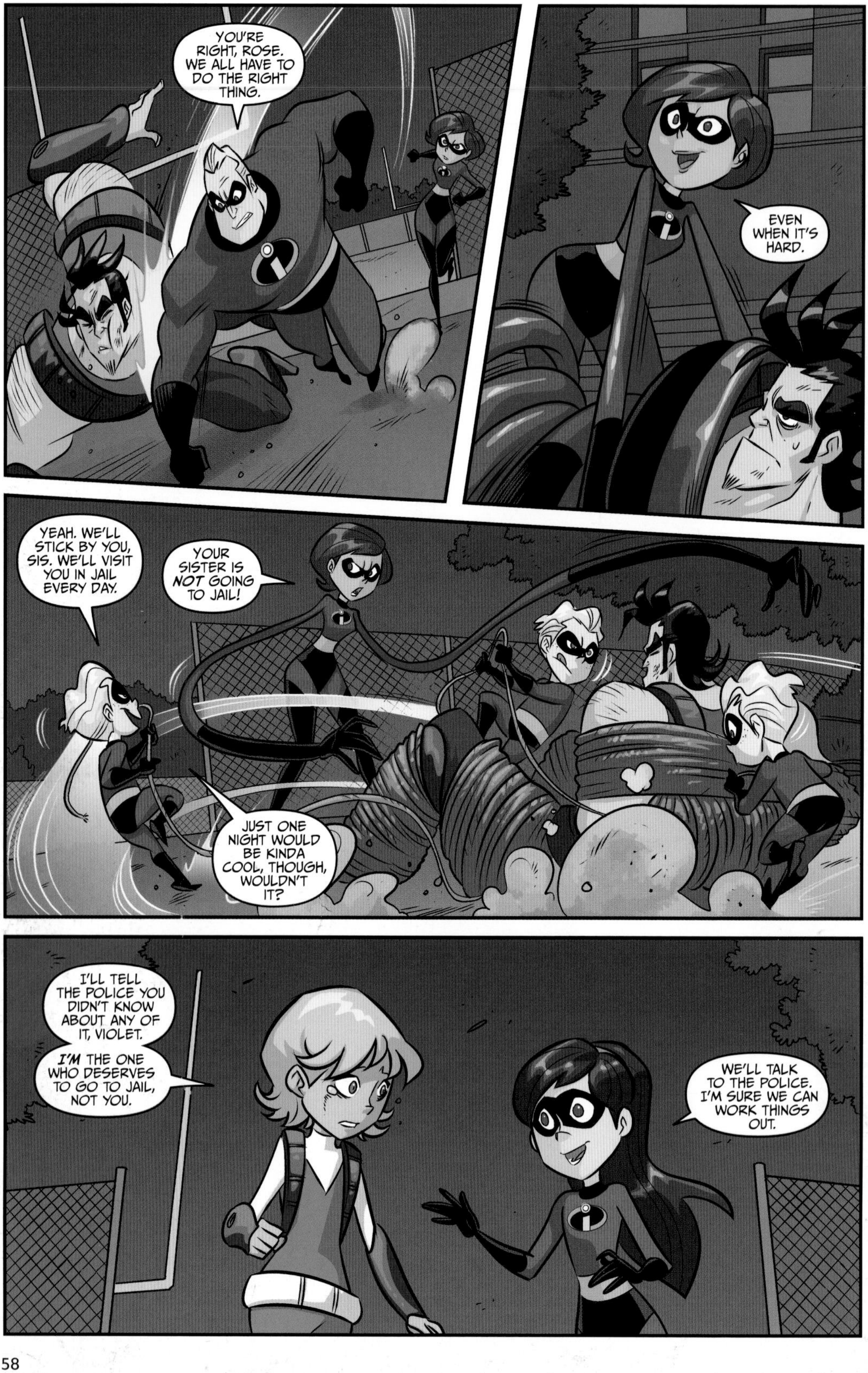

YOU'RE RIGHT, ROSE. WE ALL HAVE TO DO THE RIGHT THING.
EVEN WHEN IT'S HARD.
YEAH. WE'LL STICK BY YOU, SIS. WE'LL VISIT YOU IN JAIL EVERY DAY.
YOUR SISTER IS *NOT* GOING TO JAIL!
JUST ONE NIGHT WOULD BE KINDA COOL, THOUGH, WOULDN'T IT?
I'LL TELL THE POLICE YOU DIDN'T KNOW ABOUT ANY OF IT, VIOLET.
I'M THE ONE WHO DESERVES TO GO TO JAIL, NOT YOU.
WE'LL TALK TO THE POLICE. I'M SURE WE CAN WORK THINGS OUT.

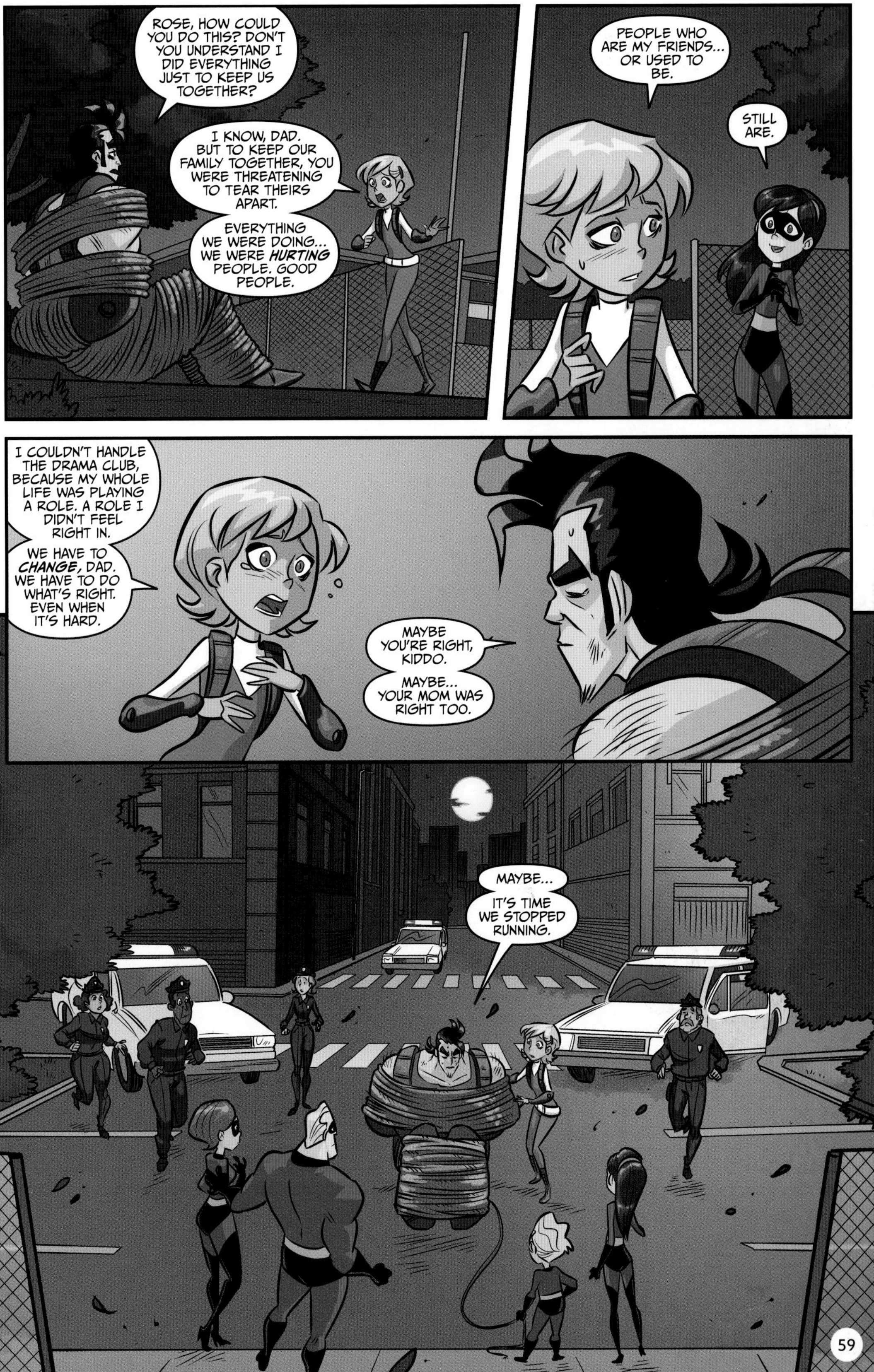

ROSE, HOW COULD YOU DO THIS? DON'T YOU UNDERSTAND I DID EVERYTHING JUST TO KEEP US TOGETHER?
I KNOW, DAD. BUT TO KEEP OUR FAMILY TOGETHER, YOU WERE THREATENING TO TEAR THEIRS APART.
EVERYTHING WE WERE DOING... WE WERE HURTING PEOPLE. GOOD PEOPLE.
PEOPLE WHO ARE MY FRIENDS... OR USED TO BE.
STILL ARE.
I COULDN'T HANDLE THE DRAMA CLUB, BECAUSE MY WHOLE LIFE WAS PLAYING A ROLE. A ROLE I DIDN'T FEEL RIGHT IN.
WE HAVE TO CHANGE, DAD. WE HAVE TO DO WHAT'S RIGHT. EVEN WHEN IT'S HARD.
MAYBE YOU'RE RIGHT, KIDDO.
MAYBE... YOUR MOM WAS RIGHT TOO.
MAYBE... IT'S TIME WE STOPPED RUNNING.

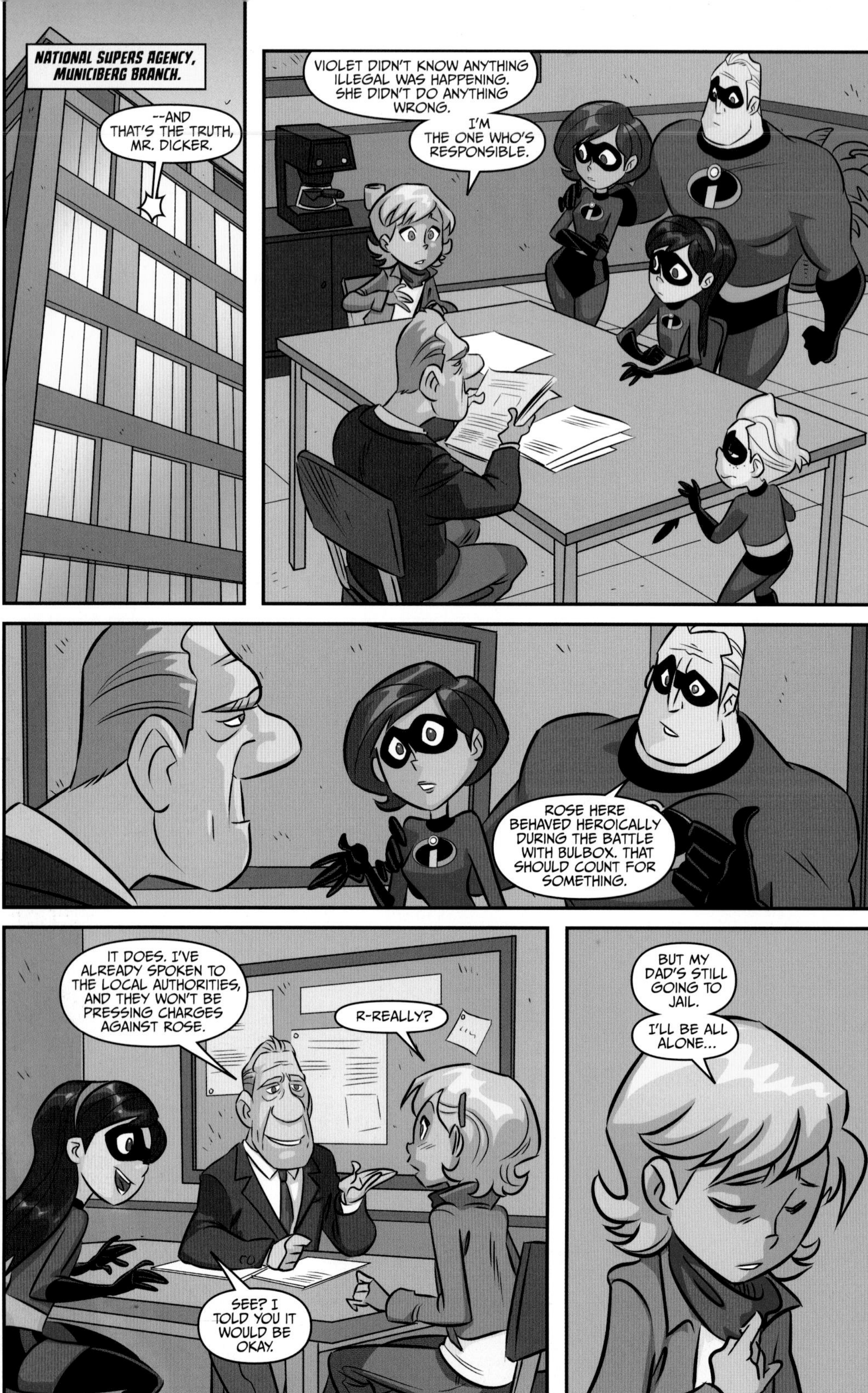
NATIONAL SUPERS AGENCY, MUNICIBERG BRANCH.
--AND THAT'S THE TRUTH, MR. DICKER.
VIOLET DIDN'T KNOW ANYTHING ILLEGAL WAS HAPPENING. SHE DIDN'T DO ANYTHING WRONG.
I'M THE ONE WHO'S RESPONSIBLE.
ROSE HERE BEHAVED HEROICALLY DURING THE BATTLE WITH BULBOX. THAT SHOULD COUNT FOR SOMETHING.
IT DOES. I'VE ALREADY SPOKEN TO THE LOCAL AUTHORITIES, AND THEY WON'T BE PRESSING CHARGES AGAINST ROSE.
R-REALLY?
SEE? I TOLD YOU IT WOULD BE OKAY.
BUT MY DAD'S STILL GOING TO JAIL.
I'LL BE ALL ALONE...

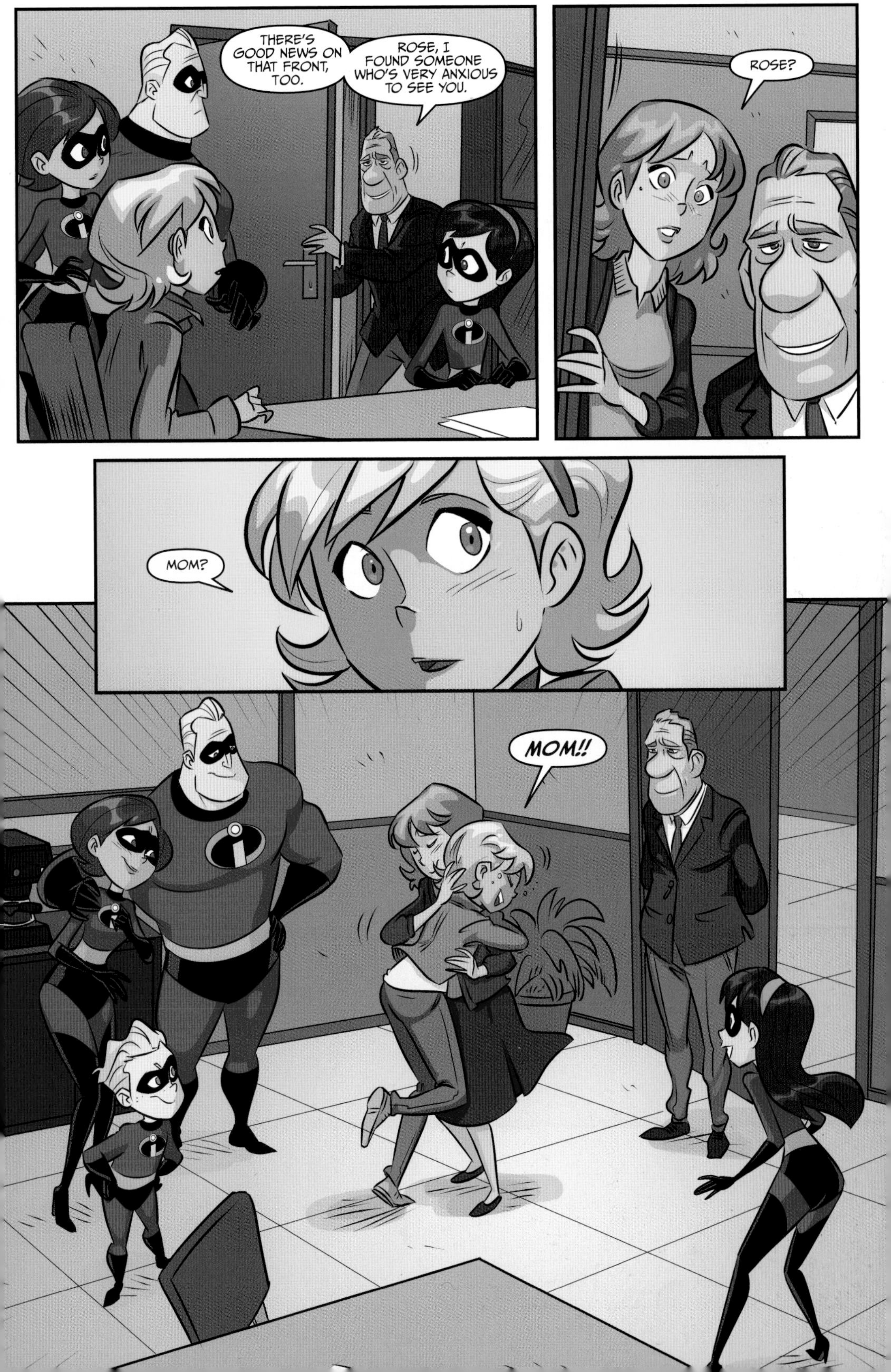
THERE'S GOOD NEWS ON THAT FRONT, TOO.
ROSE, I FOUND SOMEONE WHO'S VERY ANXIOUS TO SEE YOU.
ROSE?
MOM?
MOM!!

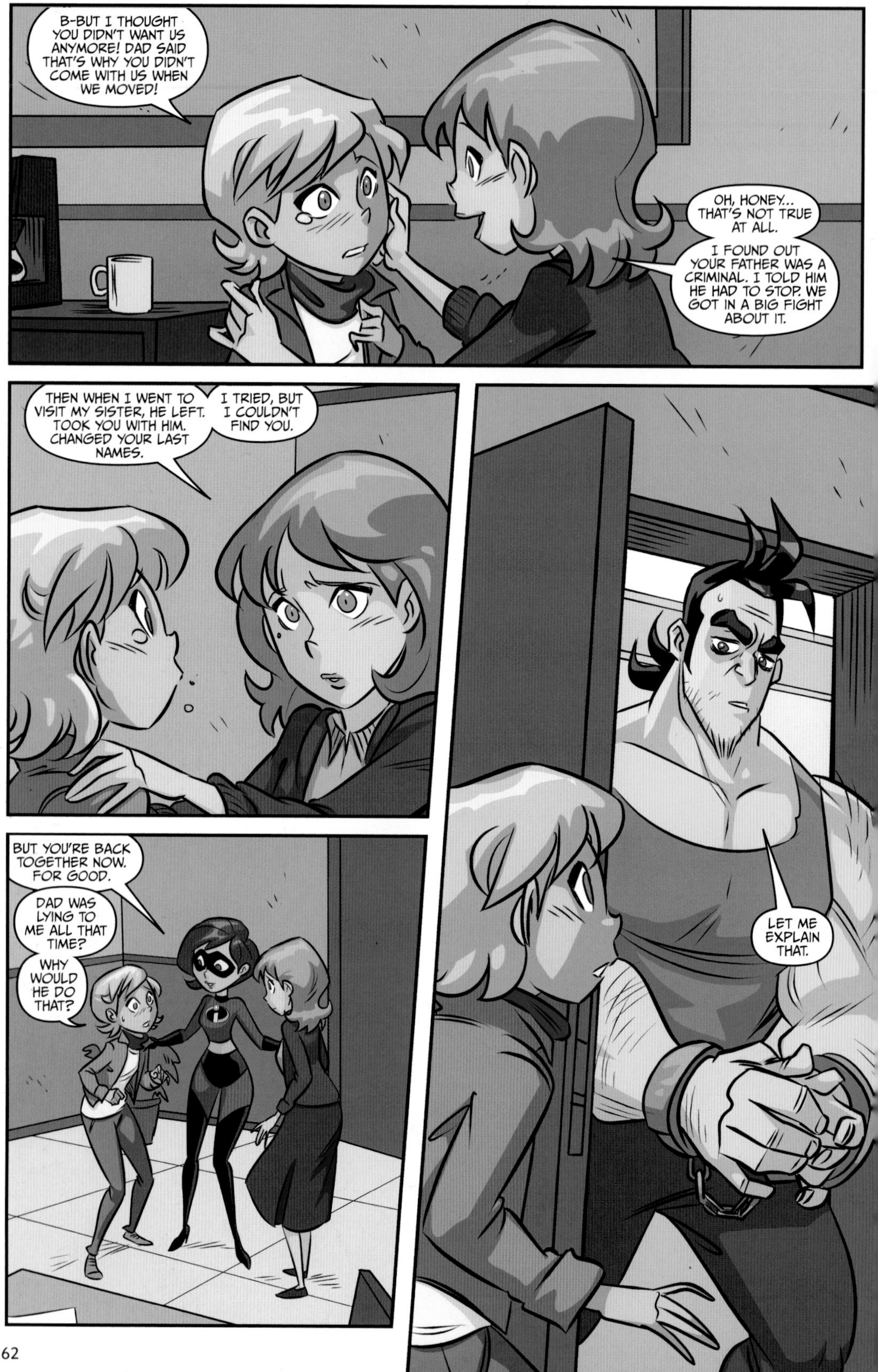
B-BUT I THOUGHT YOU DIDN'T WANT US ANYMORE! DAD SAID THAT'S WHY YOU DIDN'T COME WITH US WHEN WE MOVED!
OH, HONEY... THAT'S NOT TRUE AT ALL.
I FOUND OUT YOUR FATHER WAS A CRIMINAL. I TOLD HIM HE HAD TO STOP. WE GOT IN A BIG FIGHT ABOUT IT.
THEN WHEN I WENT TO VISIT MY SISTER, HE LEFT. TOOK YOU WITH HIM. CHANGED YOUR LAST NAMES.
I TRIED, BUT I COULDN'T FIND YOU.
BUT YOU'RE BACK TOGETHER NOW. FOR GOOD.
DAD WAS LYING TO ME ALL THAT TIME?
WHY WOULD HE DO THAT?
LET ME EXPLAIN THAT.

I'M NOT THE SMARTEST GUY IN THE WORLD. COULDN'T GET A GREAT JOB. I ALWAYS WANTED TO GIVE YOU MORE THAN I COULD.

AND WITH MY POWERS...WELL... STEALING WAS EASY.

"I TOLD MYSELF I'D ONLY DO IT ONCE. BUT THEN I DID IT AGAIN...AND AGAIN."

"THEN YOUR MOM FOUND OUT. AND THE POLICE WERE GETTING CLOSE."

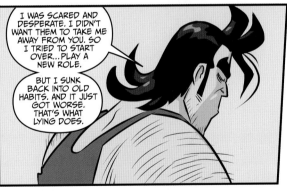

I WAS SCARED AND DESPERATE. I DIDN'T WANT THEM TO TAKE ME AWAY FROM YOU. SO I TRIED TO START OVER...PLAY A NEW ROLE.

BUT I SUNK BACK INTO OLD HABITS. AND IT JUST GOT WORSE. THAT'S WHAT LYING DOES.

CAN YOU FORGIVE ME, ROSE?

KEEP THAT PROMISE...AND I WILL.

I LOVE YOU, DADDY.

I'VE GOT TO GO TO JAIL NOW...SERVE MY TIME FOR WHAT I DID.

BUT THAT'LL GIVE ME A CLEAN SLATE...AND WHEN I GET OUT, WE CAN START OVER. I PROMISE.

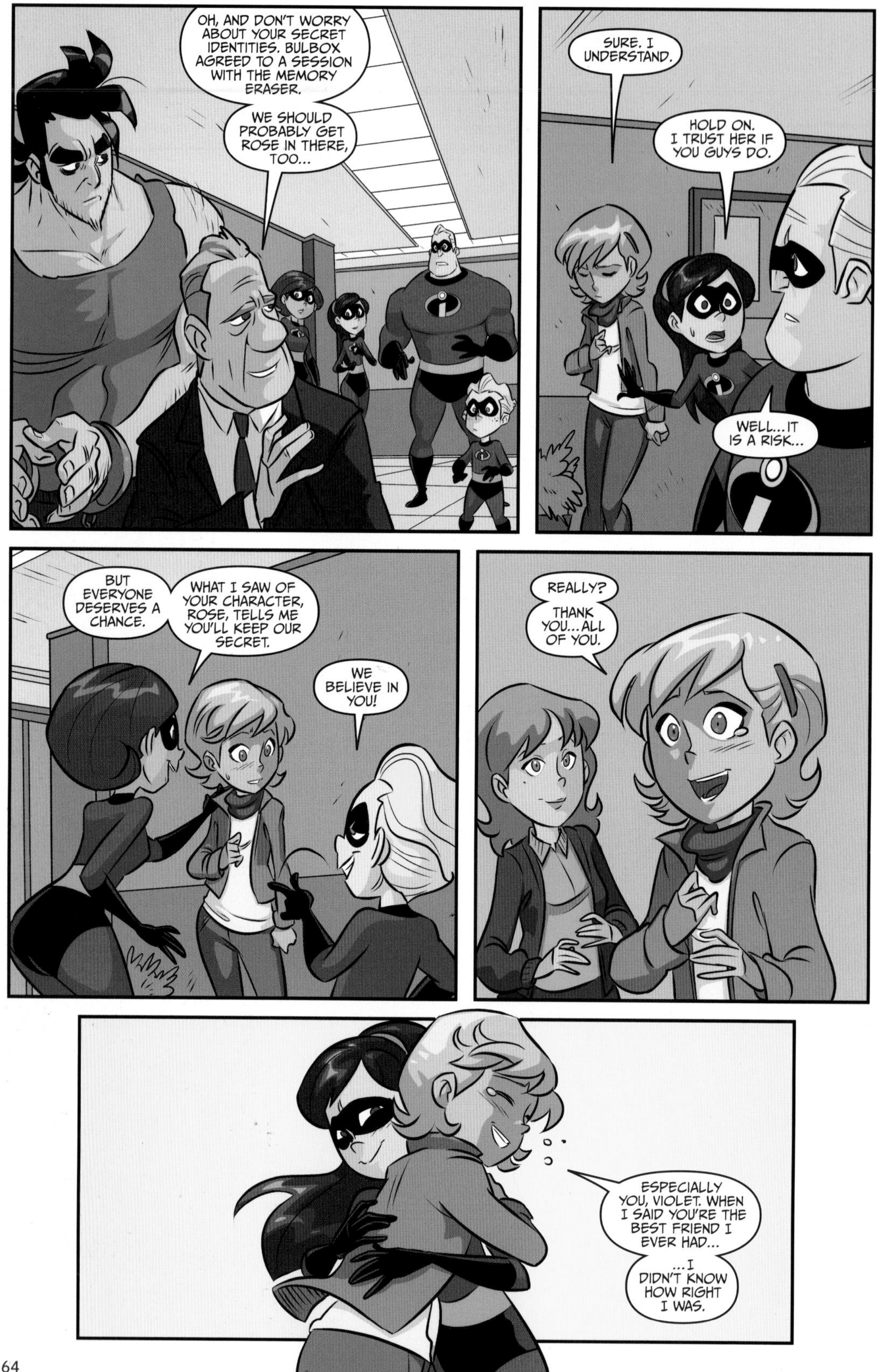

OH, AND DON'T WORRY ABOUT YOUR SECRET IDENTITIES. BULBOX AGREED TO A SESSION WITH THE MEMORY ERASER.
WE SHOULD PROBABLY GET ROSE IN THERE, TOO...
SURE. I UNDERSTAND.
HOLD ON. I TRUST HER IF YOU GUYS DO.
WELL...IT IS A RISK...
BUT EVERYONE DESERVES A CHANCE.
WHAT I SAW OF YOUR CHARACTER, ROSE, TELLS ME YOU'LL KEEP OUR SECRET.
WE BELIEVE IN YOU!
REALLY?
THANK YOU...ALL OF YOU.
ESPECIALLY YOU, VIOLET. WHEN I SAID YOU'RE THE BEST FRIEND I EVER HAD...
...I DIDN'T KNOW HOW RIGHT I WAS.

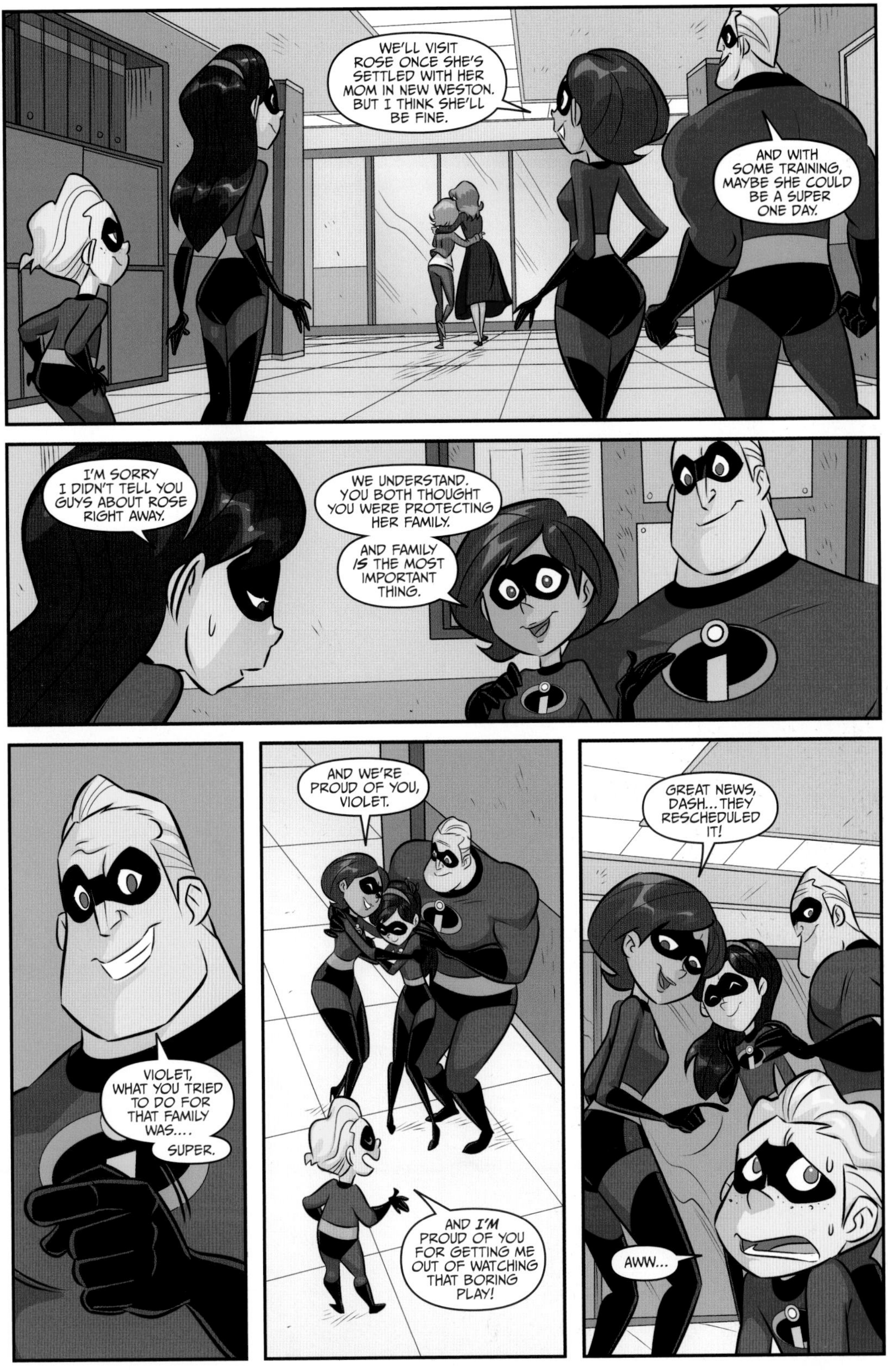
WE'LL VISIT ROSE ONCE SHE'S SETTLED WITH HER MOM IN NEW WESTON. BUT I THINK SHE'LL BE FINE.
AND WITH SOME TRAINING, MAYBE SHE COULD BE A SUPER ONE DAY.
I'M SORRY I DIDN'T TELL YOU GUYS ABOUT ROSE RIGHT AWAY.
WE UNDERSTAND. YOU BOTH THOUGHT YOU WERE PROTECTING HER FAMILY.
AND FAMILY *IS* THE MOST IMPORTANT THING.
VIOLET, WHAT YOU TRIED TO DO FOR THAT FAMILY WAS....
SUPER.
AND WE'RE PROUD OF YOU, VIOLET.
AND *I'M* PROUD OF YOU FOR GETTING ME OUT OF WATCHING THAT BORING PLAY!
GREAT NEWS, DASH... THEY RESCHEDULED IT!
AWW...

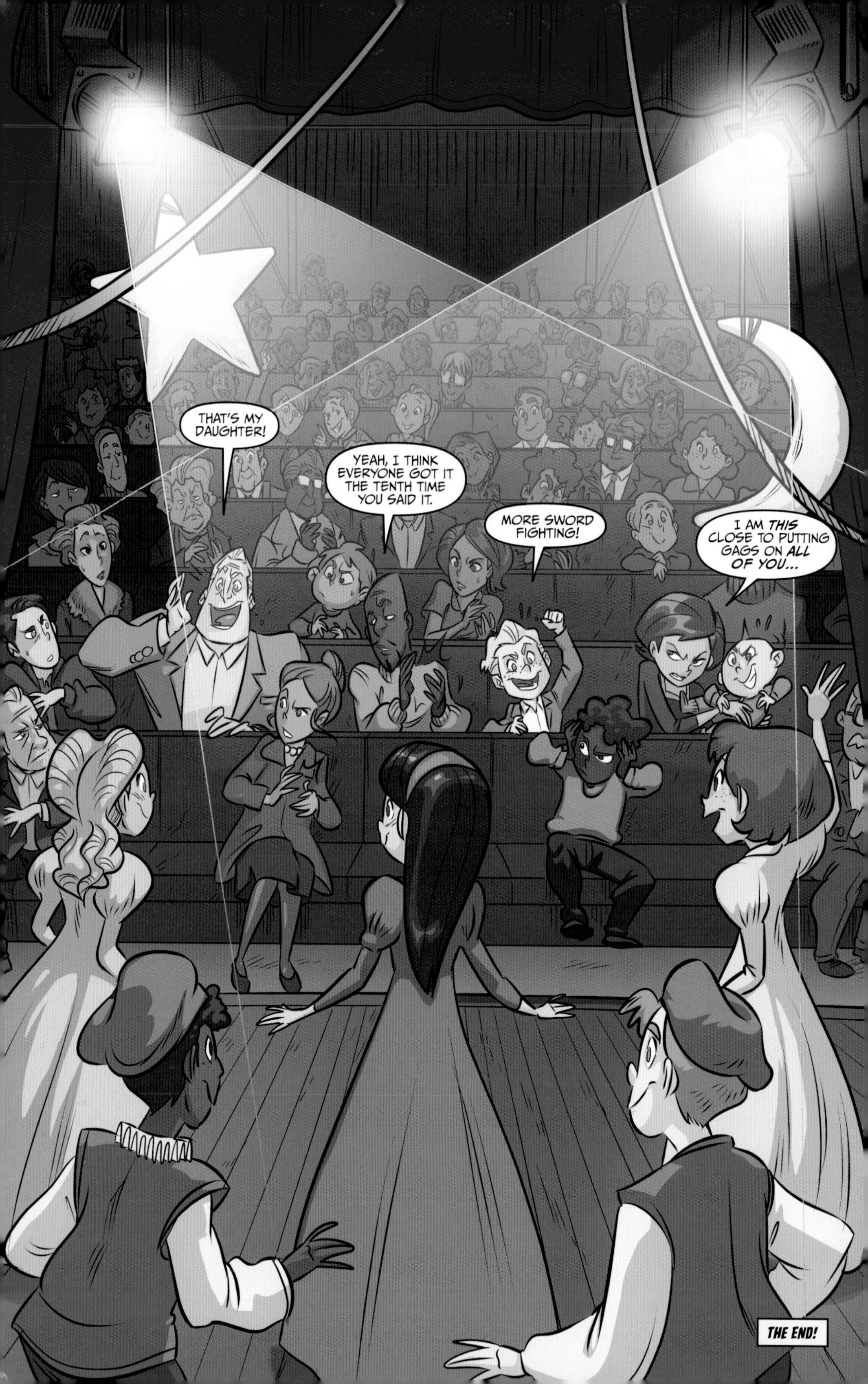
THAT'S MY DAUGHTER!
YEAH, I THINK EVERYONE GOT IT THE TENTH TIME YOU SAID IT.
MORE SWORD FIGHTING!
I AM *THIS* CLOSE TO PUTTING GAGS ON *ALL OF YOU*...
THE END!

Disney · PIXAR
INCREDIBLES 2

PIN-UP GALLERY

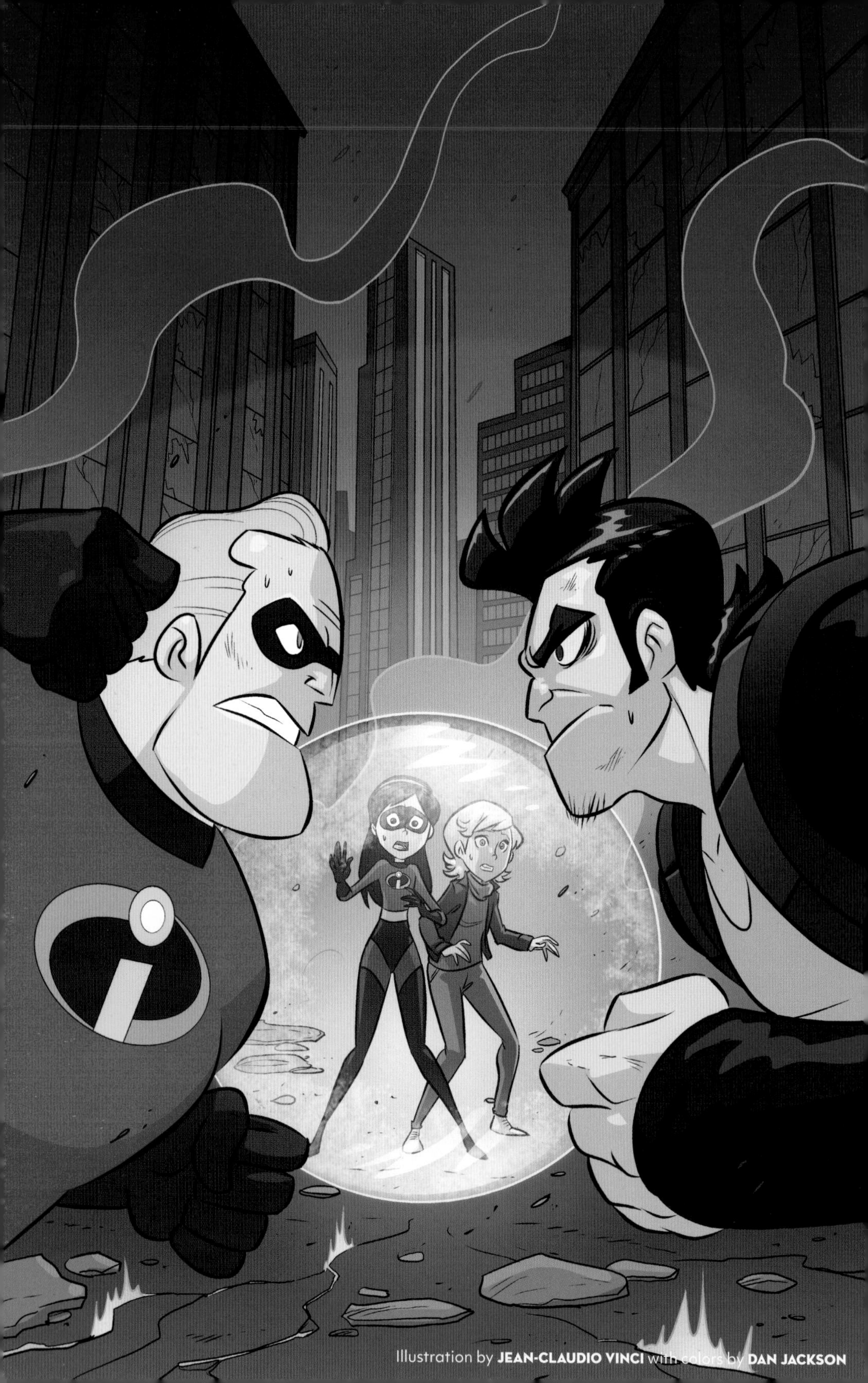

Illustration by **JEAN-CLAUDIO VINCI** with colors by **DAN JACKSON**

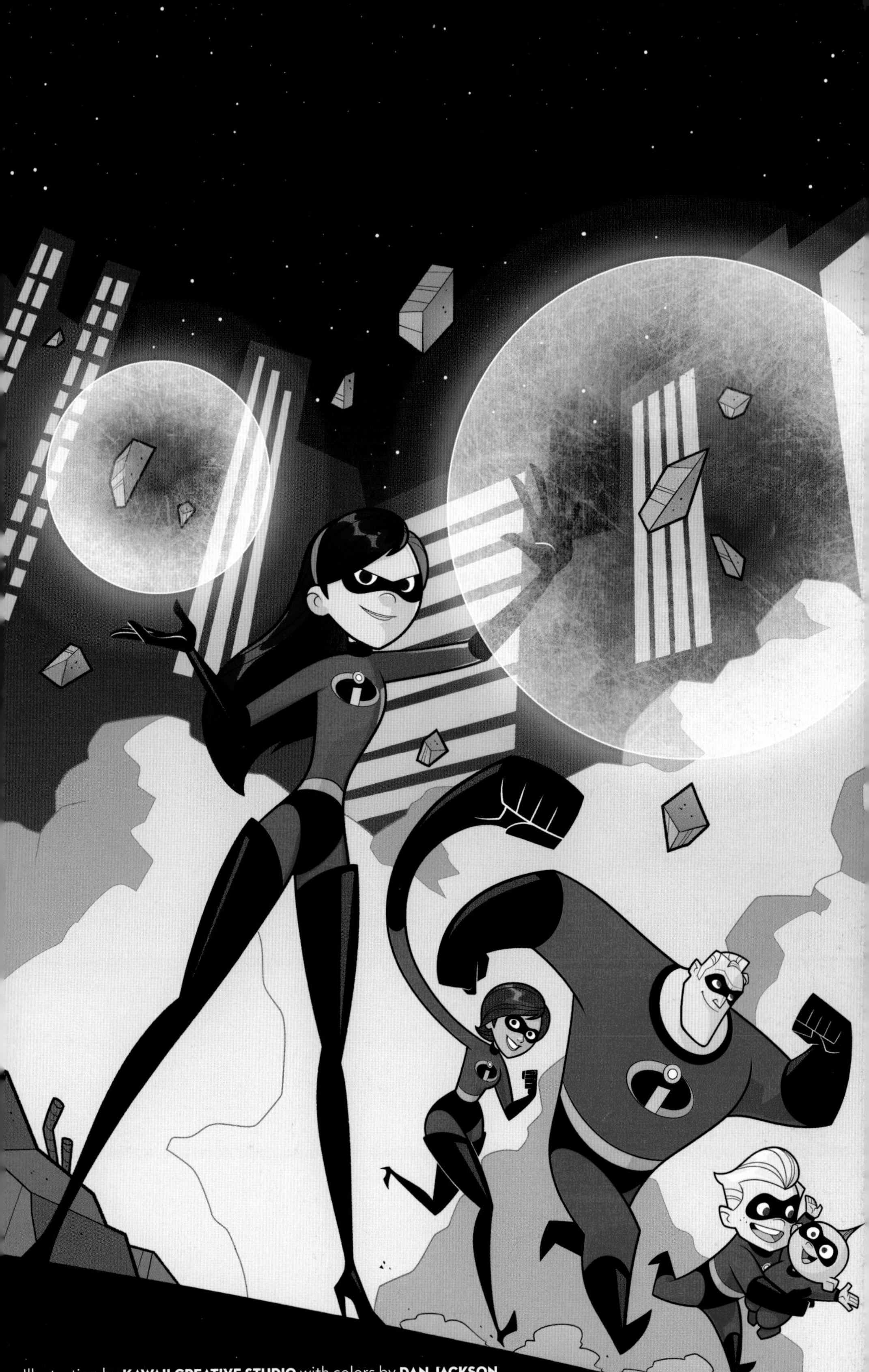

Illustration by **KAWAII CREATIVE STUDIO** with colors by **DAN JACKSON**

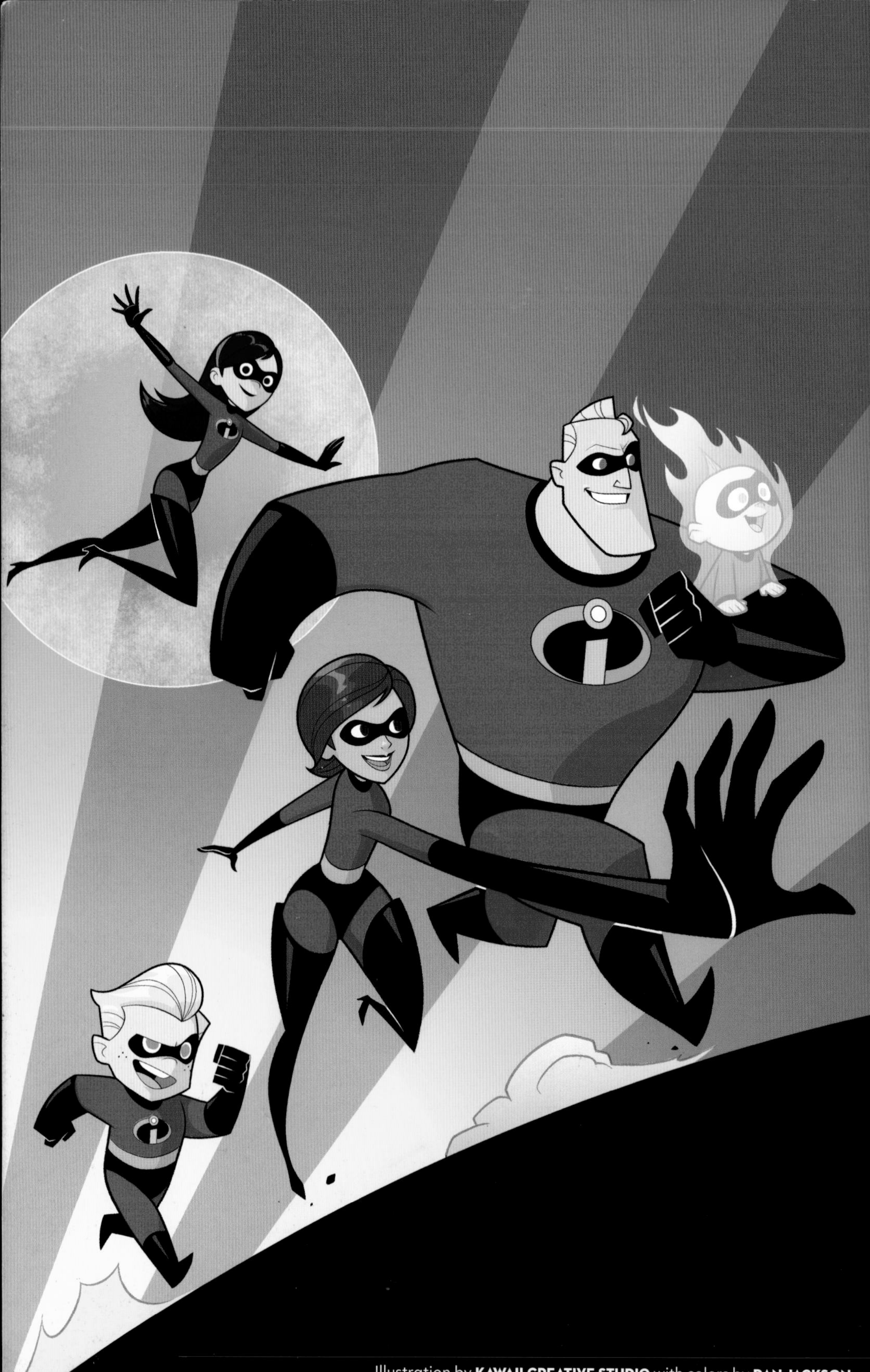

Illustration by **KAWAII CREATIVE STUDIO** with colors by **DAN JACKSON**

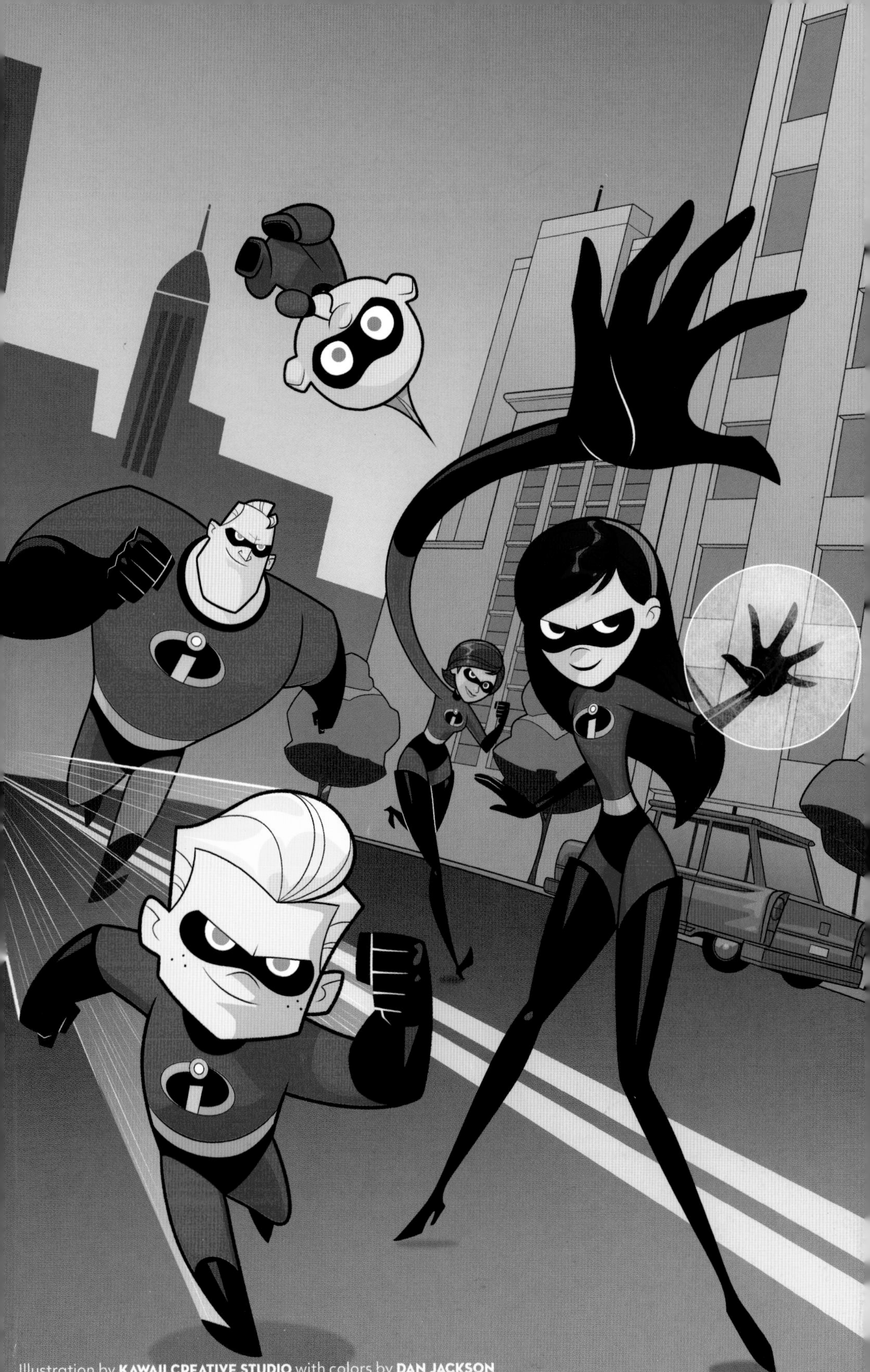

Illustration by **KAWAII CREATIVE STUDIO** with colors by **DAN JACKSON**

CATCH UP WITH DISNEY•PIXAR'S INCREDIBLES 2!

Disney · PIXAR
INCREDIBLES 2
CRISIS IN MID-LIFE! & OTHER STORIES
Disney COMICS

Disney · PIXAR
INCREDIBLES 2
CRISIS IN MID-LIFE! & OTHER STORIES

An encounter with villain Bomb Voyage inspires Bob to begin training the next generation of Supers, Dash and Violet. Mr. Incredible will find himself needing to pull his family back together . . . because Bomb Voyage is still at large! In another story, Bob tells the kids about a battle from his glory days that seems too amazing to be true—but they never imagined the details would include their mom and dad's super secret first date . . . Finally, in two adventures all his own, baby Jack-Jack and his powers are set to save the day.

978-1-50671-019-8 • $10.99

AVAILABLE AT YOUR LOCAL COMICS SHOP OR BOOKSTORE! TO FIND A COMICS SHOP IN YOUR AREA, VISIT COMICSHOPLOCATOR.COM

FOR MORE INFORMATION OR TO ORDER DIRECT: ON THE WEB: DARKHORSE.COM • EMAIL: MAILORDER@DARKHORSE.COM
PHONE: 1-800-862-0052 MON.–FRI. 9 AM TO 5 PM PACIFIC TIME

DARK HORSE BOOKS

Disney COMICS

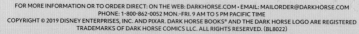